every man for herself

also by

maryann reid

Marry Your Baby Daddy

Mrs. Big

Sex and the Single Sister

Use Me or Lose Me

every man for herself

maryann reid

st. martin's griffin
new york

This is a work of fiction. All of the characters, organizations, and events portrayed in this novel are either products of the author's imagination or are used fictitiously.

 For information, address St. Martin's Press, 175 Fifth Avenue, New York, N.Y. 10010.

www.stmartins.com

Library of Congress Cataloging-in-Publication Data

Reid, Maryann.
Every man for herself / Maryann Reid.—1st ed.
p. cm.
ISBN-13: 978-0-312-36909-5
ISBN-10: 0-312-36909-3
1. African-American women—New York (State)—New York—Fiction. 2. New York (N.Y.)— Fiction. 3. Adultery—Fiction. I. Title.

PS3618.E54E94 2007
813'.6—dc22

2007016956

First Edition: September 2007

10 9 8 7 6 5 4 3 2 1

acknowledgments

This one is short and sweet, with a double shot of love.

First and foremost, I'd like to thank my mother, Veronica Reid, for being my biggest supporter and friend.

Warm hugs to my beautiful sister Arlene, my grandmother, and to each one of my friends and family who have read and purchased my books in the past. Just to name a few: Carline, Latoya, AG, Nicole, and many more.

A shout-out to the radio stations, faithful readers, bookstore managers, book clubs, and newspaper and magazine editors who read my e-mails and have taken a keen interest in my special projects.

To my agent, Richard Curtis, and my editor, Monique Patterson, for their guiding hands to a finished manuscript.

Most of all, a thank-you to God, for another blessing, and for the blessings I miss every day.

Some of us don't have relationships. We just take hostages.

—ANONYMOUS

one

"I can't breathe," Nina whispered to her friend Dee on the phone about her troubled marriage. "When he's around, I feel claustrophobic; I can't keep hiding this."

"You gotta make a move. It's either you or him," Dee sighed as they ended their phone call. Nina looked out into her crowded living room, packed with chairs from wall to wall. She counted down the minutes. Tonight, Trent's "church" service seemed to go on forever. Every Tuesday at least thirty people came to their tiny ranch home in Allswell, a backwoods town near Houston, Texas, to hear Trent spread his word. But Nina knew it was all a scam, just like his numbers, cards, and car broker businesses.

Nina silently thanked God for her meager blessings along with the rest of Trent's fan club. She asked God to help her catch her breath.

"Let us bow our heads first and thank God for the bounty in our lives. Amen," Trent said as several of his members turned around and acknowledged each other. His booming voice, thick and sweet like maple syrup, spread throughout the room. Everyone bowed in unison. "I want to conclude this service by singing a song from the Book of Hymns."

The crisp sound of turning pages filled the room as Nina ran back to the kitchen to turn off the pot of boiling water spilling onto the stove. She wrapped her blue, stained apron around her jeans and pink fitted top. Not exactly an outfit for a pastor's wife, but in her book, Trent was no pastor. She got the plates of food ready to serve to the guests when the service was done. Beads of boiling water burned her delicate brown hands as she moved the hot cast-iron pot off the stove. She had forgotten what she had boiled the water for. Cooking wasn't exactly her calling. She blasted the faucet to drown out everyone's crooning and bad notes.

She just wanted to get to the good part, the blessings. The singing and the organ music went on and on. Finally, when the song ended, Trent's deep, hazel eyes looked intently into the crowded room. He walked down the middle as heads turned, dabbing his wet, thin, mustached mouth with a handkerchief. He was well put together in a powder blue, pin-striped suit, a jacket that reached his knees, and white wing-tipped shoes with gold buckles. Nina thought he looked more pimp than holy with his nappy, curly hair combed back, but it was Trent. Too bad, she told herself, that he was so good in bed, or she would've left him a long time ago.

Trent walked back to the front of the room and fiddled with his gold cuff links. He looked at the brown palette of patient faces and said, "Look to your neighbor on your right and ask him, 'How much is getting to know the Lord really worth?' "

Nina peered over the kitchen counter as the voices rose and fell with each person asking the other. This was the part where Trent cashed in. He disguised it all under the name of God. He was already charging ten dollars at the door. Cash only.

"Now, ask yourselves in silence," Trent demanded in that sweet, syrupy tone that seemed more good than its evil intention. He folded and slipped his initial-printed handkerchief back in his jacket pocket. "Ask yourselves if you gave enough tonight in your offering? Or are you still holding back from the Lord!" he yelled, raising his hands over his head. He stomped his feet, and some folks shouted in agreement. A hat was passed around as everyone threw in spare change and many dollars.

Nina rolled her crescent-shaped eyes and carefully took the smoked turkey wings out of the pot one by one. She placed them on individual plastic plates, next to white rice. She mixed a new pitcher of lemonade and poured some in small paper cups. Thirty plates waited on the kitchen counter. This was what she had done every week for the last six months because Trent wanted to justify the money he charged at the door. She wanted no more part in his game, she thought to herself, as she carefully placed the food on the plates.

Trent said a final prayer and thanked everyone for coming. Each person got up and made their way to the kitchen counter. They picked up their plates of food and drink, some elbowing the others with a smile. Nina was courteous as usual, making sure people had enough napkins and that Brother Page had extra gravy. As everyone ate, including Trent, Nina snuck into the bedroom. She closed the door and prayed. She breathed in as far as she could, but the dampness in the air got stuck in her lungs. It was a warm summer evening and the whole place felt like a sauna. She breathed again, this time slower. She wanted to escape him, and the shit was about to hit the fan. Before she could get her prayer words together, Trent knocked.

"Baby, come on out here! Everybody's getting ready to leave. Come on out," Trent said through the door.

When Nina walked out, she saw Trent standing by the front door holding a small paper cup of water. She stood by him, as she always did.

"Sister Pearl, make sure you take some extra wings home with you," Nina said, smiling at the short, husky woman with the curly, orange-red wig.

"Thank you, Sister Raines. I sure did take some. They are good! The rice was a little sticky, but God bless you," she said as she walked out.

Nina wiped her sweaty, tired hands on her behind and faked a grin.

". . . In Jesus's name," Trent said as he sprinkled his holy water over Sister Pearl. He did the same to each person who passed. Everyone thought that Trent's holy water was blessed. If they only knew that the water came from the pipe, Nina thought as she watched Trent's antics. When they left, Nina had a big mess of pots and pans to clean up. Trent didn't help. As always, he disappeared to the basement to count his money.

Before Nina headed off to wash the dishes, she recalled her conversation with Dee, and decided to make use of her free time. *To hell with the dishes.* Nina crept back into the bedroom.

Lately, she'd been having questions about the thousands of dollars Trent had been making. She hadn't seen a dime. Bills were going unpaid. He was all decked out, and the last thing she bought herself was older than her three-year-old burgundy nail polish. They did better when she had a part-time job at the doctor's office, a job that paid for her massage therapy courses, a job that Trent thought was too "hands on" for a married woman.

There were some rumors around town that he was loaded, but why was she the last to know? She started to do some digging. She didn't know what she was looking for, but she wanted to find anything—receipts, money, or deposit slips. She searched their closet high and low and found nothing. She looked under the mattress, nothing. But there was one place that Trent had no idea she knew about. It was his sock drawer. Nina plowed through his drawer until she felt a sock that had more than just cotton in it. She untied the sock and found a stack of papers stuffed inside. Nina listened to see if she could hear Trent, but everything was quiet. She expected him to be in the basement for at least another half hour. She locked the bedroom door with a click, sat on the bed, and unfolded her find. Her eyes raced over the words on the paper. It didn't make sense. She saw figures like "500,000" and words like "asset" and "real property." When she finally put it all together, Nina discovered that Trent was holding out on her. He had five hundred thousand dollars in savings in several bank accounts from property he had bought and sold over the last year, not to mention an equivalent amount in equity from property he was renting. He was writing everything off under his guise as a preacher. It was never about the Lord.

Nina crumpled the papers in her fist. "He lied," she said into the thin air. He was leading another life she had no clue about, while they ate crumbs and she wore the same clothes day in and out. All the accounts were in his name so she would not have known. This devastated her. She wondered what else she didn't know about Trent, and if she even wanted to be around to find out. Then she heard him coming.

"Hot damn! Eight hundred dollars tonight! Amen!" yelled Trent as he laughed and put the money in a clip on the wall unit.

Nina didn't respond as she stuffed the papers back in the sock drawer and walked to the kitchen where he was, sticking his head in the fridge.

"You know what, baby?" he said, his T-shirt pulled up halfway and showing off his round, brown belly. He slapped Nina's behind as she walked by him. "I think I may raise the price by a dollar or two. With this money, I can buy you a new Chevy. What do you think?"

Nina didn't look at him, but at the clock that read 10 P.M. "I don't want a new Chevy."

He pressed his weight against her behind. "Mmm, what you want then?" he whispered in her ear. "A baby?"

Nina spun around. "Why haven't I seen any of the money?"

He backed away with a sour look. "I have it in a savings account." His light eyes blinked erratically.

"Where's the proof?"

"Proof?"

"Why do I feel you are hiding things from me? You turning into a preacher is not making our life heavenly, it's making it hell!" Nina said, her caramel-colored skin brightening with anger. She stood face-to-face with him in the kitchen.

"Come on, girl," Trent said, trying to reach out for her hand. "You know I ain't into no preaching like that. This is a business. You know we ain't never been no churchgoing folk."

"I wanna see the money in the account," Nina said, walking out of the kitchen.

Trent followed her like a puppy toward the bedroom.

Nina walked quickly to the bedroom, opened the sock drawer, and pulled out the papers. "This is called fraud. We can go to jail taking these folks' money. Not to mention what else I don't know!"

Trent sat on the bed. "You went through my things?"

"What are you hiding, Trent? You haven't worked a job for more than a year. Every year it's a new thing. What's next after this, a strip joint?"

Trent scratched his head like it was a damn good idea. "A real man don't got to explain his money to nobody. As long as I take care—"

"You don't take care of shit but Trent!" Nina sneered, her eyes as narrow as a keyhole slit, and threw the papers at him as they scattered about the room.

"What are you doing with all that money?!"

Trent looked like he was lost. He picked up the papers piece by piece, stopping at the door. "These are some *investments* I made." He sat on the edge of the bed and lit a cigarette. "You can't even spell the word."

Nina ignored that. She wasn't about to let him deflect her, or let him get his ass out of hot water. "Why didn't I know?" Nina asked through her teeth.

"Because you wouldn't understand a damn thing about real estate. I don't want your country ass in my business, period." The cigarette dangled from Trent's thick lips as he put the papers back in his sock.

"How about I take my country ass the hell outta here and leave yours in the dust heap," Nina said as she stormed out of the house.

"Go on then, you still ain't got nothing without me!" she heard him shout.

Nina jumped in their battered black pickup truck for a long ride. She didn't have much, but she had her power and will. She dialed Dee's number and asked for a ride in the morning.

two

By the next morning, Nina was packing her bags. She was spending the next few nights at her mama's house while she planned her next move. She wanted to make sure she had everything; she wasn't leaving unprepared. Her discount, generic facial creams, day and night clothes, and other knickknacks were positioned neatly and tightly into her bags. She wasn't quite sure what her next move was gonna be. It was clear that the marriage was over. They were no longer partners, but in each other's way. Her heart was pounding at what lay ahead as Trent slept in the next room. Today was Trent's birthday, and she knew she'd better leave before he remembered that he was turning forty-three today. If it wasn't for her, he'd forget when to shit. He was always forgetful about everything, including their marriage vows. She parted the door and gazed at him lying there, face up. It took her last rational nerve to not want to pour a pot of icy water all over his naked body. But she had to move quick. It was already 7:30 A.M. Her girl Dee was picking her up.

Nina noticed some headlights outside and realized Dee had come a little early. That only meant that Dee had breakfast on her mind. Nina pulled back the yellow cotton curtain and saw Dee flashing a grin. Nina quickly braided her hair into a ponytail and wrote Trent a brief Dear John letter, leaving it at his bedside. She slipped out the door and dumped her bags in the trunk of Dee's creamy Lexus sedan. Dee had bought it for her husband, but drove it more than he did. She was on husband number three, and had four children. It was hard to keep up with Dee, Nina thought as she slid into the cream-colored leather passenger seat. But of all the people Nina knew in her small town, Dee was the only one Nina liked, because she liked Nina.

"Girrl, I can eat a whole pot of grits, never mind a few spoonfuls," Dee said as the both laughed for no reason, but in total agreement.

They drove twenty minutes down the road to Jake's Place, a quaint red-painted diner with a blue awning. They sat at a booth at the back of the diner and ordered grits, eggs, bacon, toast, and a pitcher of orange juice.

"So," Dee said as she situated her big hands on the table. "Did you tell him?"

"I did. It's over. Especially after what I found."

"What could be worse than what you was living in?" Dee said.

"I found out that he's been hiding thousands of dollars from me. He had some papers stuffed away in his drawer. His forgetful ass probably meant to move them, but thank God he didn't."

"Is he crazy? That man could be living some other life and you just his front," Dee said, her rounded mouth open in a perfect circle. She started waving her blue manicured fingers in the air. "I read all the time how men like that be disappearing, leaving their families to fend for themselves. Nina, you had nothing. You didn't even have any security."

"I got my security now," Nina said, adjusting her black, cotton stretch tank top. "And it's me."

"Girl, look at you," Dee said, slapping the table as her gold bangles jingled. "Now, that's the tune you shoulda been singing all along."

They both laughed and grinned as the healthy platter of bacon, grits, toast, and fried eggs was set down by the shy, pimple-faced Hispanic waiter.

"And I'm so glad I did it today, on his birthday," Nina said as she watched Dee push her black, shiny dreadlocks off her shoulder. "Fool didn't even notice. Just glad I don't have to spend it looking in his face again. No romance, no dinners, nothing."

"Well, when I told my second husband, Larry, on our anniversary, it was the best thing I ever done. Couldn't have picked a better day. I swooped down on that ass on a day he didn't expect and saved a lot of money, too," Dee said, her gold bangles making music as she moved her hands over the table for the salt and pepper.

"I remember that day, and I remember how he put you in the hospital," Nina recalled. She spread some blueberry jam on her toast. Dee's second husband had chased her out of the house with a knife until Dee fell in a sinkhole outside their house.

Dee grimaced as she thought back, too. "And I still think it was the best day of my life."

They ate in silence for a few moments as they both descended into their breakfast bliss of warm, home-cooked food that soothed their souls.

"You know," Nina said as she looked around the diner and saw that little by little the booths were being filled with more chatter and customers. "Trent and I were simply going in two separate directions. He had money and security, and I didn't. He acted like I wasn't even important. He made decisions by himself. We had no benefits and the house we lived in was rented out and owned by my mama. I was just plain tired."

"I know how it feels to be unsatisfied. I don't weigh 275 pounds for nothing," Dee said as she cooled her grits with her full, deep orange-painted lips. "I never feel full whether it's food or happiness. But right now, in my life," Dee said, taking a bite out of the toast in her right hand, "I really think Walter is the one. He's made me the happiest."

"You've been married for almost two years. Now that's a record for you!" Nina squirted some ketchup on her fried eggs. Walter was a dark-skinned, tall, pretty boy with curly hair and Dee's current husband. He was twenty-three, thirteen years younger, too.

"The sex has been good with all my husbands. But Walter and I get down and dirty. I mean, he is into everything, including my back fat and belly rolls."

Nina smiled and admired Dee's fitted red and yellow dress. Dee was a big girl with a waist and a shape. But Nina was confused. "So, is it just about sex?"

"Oh, no, not at all. We love each other, too. And he's nothing like Larry. Damn, Larry and I were married for five years and had sex like five times. He was just around like a damn plant that I fertilized when I felt like it."

Nina laughed. She knew Dee could be a hoot when she wanted to. "I just wanna be happy, Dee. Trent was trying to get me pregnant. I couldn't bring no babies into that madness. I don't want any kids at all, ever. Another reason why it would've never worked."

"Listen," Dee said as she touched Nina's hand. "You may meet a man who can change all that. You may want to have kids with him. Being with a good man has a way of making the world look brighter, friendlier."

Nina chewed her food in contemplation. The last thing on her mind was having children, but she felt she had enough years to make up her mind. She was only twenty-five. She liked the idea of being with a man who could change things. She knew she had to change herself, first. Nina and Dee finished their plates as they got lost in the clinking and clapping sounds of plates and utensils and heightened chatter as the diner filled up with early churchgoers.

"What are your plans?" Dee finally asked Nina.

"I'm gonna stay with my mama—"

"Is that where I'm supposed to be driving you to?" Dee asked with a screwed-up face. "Girl, you know she is just two doors down from where y'all live. You'll find yourself back with Trent in no time."

"That's not true. I need time to think—"

"That's bull, Nina. You are half stepping. What are you scared of?"

"Failing. I don't have enough money. The last thing I want is to camp out at my crazy mama's house with Mr. Darrell. But I—"

"What would you do if you had the money and no fears?" Dee asked as she leaned forward.

A smile crossed Nina's lips. "I'd move to New York City in a heartbeat." But Nina waved the idea away. "But it's too far—"

"Nina, I know this is scary, but you gotta jump for your life, baby. You gotta be aggressive and let Trent know you mean business. You are young, and don't need to be in this backward town. You don't want to end up like me."

Nina looked at Dee and for the first time saw the sadness. It was an unspoken agreement between them. No need to explain, Nina thought. She knew Dee would've done things different if she could've.

"I want to meet new people, eat in bed, sleep late, go out to a club—"

"Or two—" Dee grinned. "Live your life. If I could go to a new city and no one knew me, I'd be anybody I wanted to be. You can do that."

Nina thought some more. All her bags were packed. But how could she go to New York now? She at least needed a ticket, she said to herself.

"I really do want to be as far away from Trent as possible. God knows that the police could be knocking on our door any day," Nina said as she wrung her hands together, nervous.

"How about I help you?" Dee asked.

"You have already—" Nina said, not wanting this moment to end. She knew the sooner they left the diner, the sooner she'd have to decide. Now, going to her mama's house seemed foolish.

Dee took out her green leather purse. "I have some connections in New York that can get you a place, maybe a job. But if you go, you gonna need some cash."

Nina's eyes bugged out as she watched Dee open her checkbook and write a check for five thousand dollars. She knew Dee was well-off financially since her lingerie business took off a few years ago. Nina admired her for that because she wanted to open up a massage business in the future. She hoped one day she could do for somebody else what Dee was doing for her.

"It ain't much, but it can get you a modest apartment until you start working or find you a good man!"

Nina took the check from Dee almost too quickly. She counted the zeros to be sure and kissed the check. "Thank you! You know I will pay you back."

"Don't worry about the money this time. We're like sisters. Just promise me that you will not let Trent fuck with ya head."

"Never," Nina assured her and the words never rang more true. She took a sip of her nearly-finished orange juice. "There's a train leaving for New York every day."

"How do you know?" Dee asked, folding her arms on the table.

"I checked online a few weeks ago. I was just playing around with the computer." Nina had almost forgotten she did that.

"And you're all packed?"

"Yup." Nina nodded. "But can I go now?"

"Bitch, you better go after I done give you some money!" Dee laughed as her dreads shook back and forth with her neck movement.

Nina laughed, too. It was already happening. Her life was changing. She was going to New York.

"Come on, now, let's stop all this sweet talk," Dee said, pulling out her cell phone. "Your mama pushed you into this marriage when you were way too young. And we know why she did that. It wasn't out of love. I don't want you ending up like these bamma girls. I want you to get your own thing, be independent. Then get a good man. Know what I mean?"

Nina took the phone from Dee and Dee slipped her one of her credit cards. She could hardly dial information fast enough to get the digits for Amtrak. In a matter of minutes, she had booked a ticket to her new life.

But there was one more piece of business at hand: her mama's birthday party. Yes, Trent and her mama had the same birthday.

three

Before Nina arrived at her mother's house, she wanted to pay a final visit to her father's grave. Nina's father, Errol Pickens, was buried a few miles from where Nina grew up. As Dee waited, she walked over the short hill to her father's resting place. She tried to visit him at least twice a year. There was a dense morning fog covering the ground, and dew dripped from hanging branches. It was only February, but the air was cool, not cold, with an easy breeze. Nina thought that the gray, quiet morning didn't fit the joy she felt inside since her breakfast with Dee earlier. But that took a back position as she thought about her daddy. Mr. Pickens was a rolling stone. He'd been just as tall as her mama, ruggedly handsome, and had eyes that spoke more than his mouth. He was her father, but also everybody else's, at least one or two across town. Despite his cheating ways, Nina loved her father more than she loved herself. She could see why women could not leave him alone. He had a way of turning every woman's imperfection around. Blind women, women with children, obese women, facially scarred women, and beautiful women—all were her daddy's admirers. Even after her daddy would break off the relationship, they'd walk around town praising him. He was funny, too. Sometimes, Nina's mother would be yelling at him loud enough so that the high heavens would shiver, and the next moment Nina would see her crack half a smile. Nina wasn't the prettiest little girl. She had two poles for legs and a plain face, but he made her feel like a beauty. "Hey, Gorgeous," he would say.

As Nina stood over his grave with the wind sweeping her chin-length hair, she tried to put words together to make sense of her father's death. Even though he cheated on her mother, he always made Nina feel like the number one woman in his life. Maybe her mother resented that, she thought. He would drop everything to hear what she had done with her day or even look at a silly picture she had painted. Sometimes, he'd even take her to the neighborhood bar where he would meet some of his "lady friends." She would sit in the back and play cards with Uncle Tommy and his wife. He never left Nina's sight and always made sure she was safe. Nina would keep his secrets, too. She thought about how she actually liked doing that, because it meant her mother wouldn't have to yell at him.

Nina looked down at his beautifully kept grave and placed her bunch of red roses next to a bushel of fresh sunflowers that were already there. She realized it was from another woman, because her mother hadn't visited her father's grave since she had put him in the ground ten years ago. Nina walked back down the green-covered hill to Dee. Her heels stuck from time to time in the moist dirt, making her walk slower. As she drove away, she watched her father's engraved headstone disappear.

• • •

If Nina lived in the backwater part of town, then Nina's mother, Ms. Rona Bettus, lived in the back backwaters. It was her home and her hellhole for nine years. Ms. Bettus lived in a tiny brown ranch house surrounded by unkempt grass. The closest home was six miles away. Nina saw it from the distance as the cab drove up the hills, jumping and skidding along the rocky path. She reminded herself that after today, it was all about her. She didn't care what happened at the party, even if Trent was there. Her train was leaving first thing in the morning.

"Lord have mercy," Nina's Aunt Celia said as she opened the door. She flattened out the crease in her orange housedress embroidered with white, tiny flowers. "We didn't know when you guys would get here—"

"I'm by myself," Nina said as she walked in. Aunt Celia stood at the door looking out at the porch as if Trent was going to magically appear. Nina waited for Aunt Celia to get it together. Nina and Trent were inseparable for the last five years, and it would take a while for everyone to understand.

"Well, is he coming?" Aunt Celia asked as she closed the door.

"Not sure," Nina said, signaling that she wanted to change the subject.

Aunt Celia huffed, questioning what could be keeping Trent. Finally, she gave Nina a hug, and to Nina that was exactly what she needed right now. Aunt Celia was Nina's mother's twin sister. Nina thought it was strange for two people who were identical twins to be so different.

Nina followed Aunt Celia into the party. Aunt Celia led her into the living room where the crowd had gathered and some seventies soul music played. Her mother's home still looked the same. The plastic-covered floral furniture, the cigarette-stained carpet, and the photos of white Jesus still had their proper places. Shimmery, white and red garlands hung across the walls with a sparkling "Happy Birthday" sign. The table was set with trays of barbecued chicken wings, slices of roast beef, mac and cheese, collard greens, crab cakes, conch fritters, honeyed ham, and a luscious white coconut frosted cake. Nina's birthdays never looked this good.

When she looked to her side, Aunt Celia was gone. Immediately, Nina felt alone. People whispered in her direction. She looked decent in a plain white summer dress and sandals that Dee and she had picked up after breakfast. She wanted to leave a nice last impression on folks. Her hair was swept up in a roll with a few loose tendrils on the side that elongated her slender, elegant neck. But it wasn't about how she looked. It was about what happened to her many years ago, and the lies her mother had told. Nina didn't recognize any of these people, but they all seemed to recognize her. A sudden tinge of missing Trent surprised her. At least she'd have someone to talk to. She stood in the center of the room, holding her purse, trying to stake out a good place to park herself. She smiled awkwardly at people; some smiled back, others didn't. She had never been close to her family because of her mother, but was doing her best to be nice.

Nina wandered to a quiet corner, when she saw her mother dancing with Mr. Darrell in the kitchen. His face was resting on her massive breasts. She was a large woman, about six feet, over two hundred pounds. When Nina was a child, she used to have nightmares about her. But with all that height and weight, her mother was a beauty. Her wide, light brown eyes, curvy hips, and perfectly situated nose looked like they had been carved by the hands of an expert sculptor. A slicked-back look with a long, swinging, thick ponytail was her signature hairdo. Her deep, dark, brown skin was even and coated her body like molasses.

Nina stood at the kitchen doorway. But as usual, no one seemed to notice. Her mother just kept on dancing. *Mr. Darrell still comes first,* Nina thought. When it came to him, it was like no one else in the world mattered. He was Nina's stepfather, about five feet eleven, 240 pounds, and had several tattoos on his right arm. He was twenty years younger than Ms. Bettus and that made him thirty-two, younger than Trent and much more akin to Nina's age. He and Ms. Bettus had been together for ten years. After Nina's father died in a choking incident—rumor said a hex was put on him by a town woman he had cheated with—Ms. Bettus didn't miss a beat. She got on with Mr. Darrell soon after. Nina was fifteen, and he was twenty-one. She made Nina call him "Mr. Darrell," thinking that would draw the line between the two. Unfortunately, Mr. Darrell crossed that line. The only thing Nina respected about him was that he didn't beat her mama like her father had.

"Hi, Mama," Nina said as she stood at the kitchen entrance. It had been weeks since they had spoken because she usually called the house to speak to Trent.

Ms. Bettus turned around with a shot of whiskey in her right hand. "Hey, honey," she said, still doing the two-step with Mr. Darrell. He didn't even look Nina's way. Finally, Mr. Darrell let go of Nina's mother and Nina walked over to her. She wanted to talk to her mother about everything going on like a daughter was supposed to. Even at her age, Nina still held many secrets. She couldn't even dare tell her mother about divorcing Trent and going to New York. If she did, it just wouldn't happen.

Her mother gave her a weak, one-armed hug. "You really could've helped me out with your husband's party," she said, swinging her ponytail off her shoulder.

"Mama, you told me you wanted to do it, like the year before, and the year before that," Nina reminded her. It was as if her mother was running out of stuff to criticize her about, Nina thought. Nina was not in the mood today to be anyone's joke.

"I guess I forgot," Ms. Bettus said, cutting her eyes at Nina. "Did you forget your manners?" She looked at Nina and then at Mr. Darrell.

"Hi, Mr. Darrell," Nina said, looking away at the table covered with several more aluminum trays of food. "Can I help with anything?" Nina asked, starting to feel the heat in the kitchen.

"You lookin' mighty nice today for a change," Mr. Darrell said, grinning with his yellow, gold-capped teeth. He rolled up behind Ms. Bettus and tickled her belly. They laughed like high school lovers. "Your mama been up all night slavin'."

"It wasn't over the food," Nina mumbled to herself.

"Excuse me?" Ms. Bettus said, walking toward Nina.

"I said it must've been over the food," Nina said, just to avoid a fight. It didn't take much to stir her mother up. Mr. Darrell just stood there shaking his head.

"What needs to go outside?" Nina said, about to go off if Mr. Darrell even so much as said another word to her.

"Take that ham and platter of greens with you." Ms. Bettus gathered a few trays of her own. They set them on the table in the living room. Nina wanted to keep busy in case Trent walked in any minute.

Looking up the stairs, Ms. Bettus demanded, "Nina, get out that green tablecloth from the linen closet. These folks done messed up my good white cotton."

Nina went upstairs and didn't want to come back down. She was giving herself another half hour before she left. Though her mother and she didn't get along, it just wouldn't feel right if she missed her party. Just because her mother was one way, she thought, she could at least be the bigger person. Perhaps one day her mother would notice. As soon as she reached the top of the stairs, she heard the doorbell ring, and then a bunch of cheers. It was Trent. He was here. Nina took her sweet time looking for the cloth. She told herself when she went back downstairs that she was going to walk past him and never look back, ever. He had never been a husband to her, never protected her from Mr. Darrell's advances, and rarely took her side. In fact, she couldn't wait to see the look on his face, when she kept on moving out the door.

She leaned over the railing and saw him dressed in his blue jeans, gold shiny watch, and blue checkered shirt. He looked around, as if he was looking for her. She heard somebody say that she was upstairs. But then her mother canoodled him and dragged him into the kitchen. Nina continued on to the linen closet, passed her childhood bedroom, and felt a chill. It was as cold as ever. It was now Mr. Darrell's "office." It was a room where Nina quickly had grown into a woman, not by choice. At fifteen, Mr. Darrell tried to rape her twice. After the third time of fighting him off with her mother accusing her of lying to get rid of him, Nina ultimately just gave up. A part of her died when Mr. Darrell became her first. When she turned eighteen and was getting her period regularly, he wanted only oral sex. He called it his way of showing her how to be a woman. After she'd do him, she'd spend almost an hour over the toilet brushing her teeth. One time he made her swallow, and Nina threw up on his dick. But that didn't stop him. Sometimes after he'd eat her, she'd get horrible yeast infections. Nina thought it was her body trying to fight off every speck of his being, of whatever he put in her. If Nina hadn't married Trent she probably would've killed herself or Mr. Darrell. Her mother arranged that she marry Trent to get her out of the house for good.

Nina ran her hands across the pink paisley wallpaper and realized that some things do not change. There was also a bloodstain from her mother's head still there, now brown and dried into the paper fabric. It was where her father had repeatedly pounded her head one night. Her father, though, had never laid a hand on Nina.

Nina opened the linen closet and pulled out the first green tablecloth she saw. Then she felt a presence.

"Looking for me?" Mr. Darrell grinned, with that gold-fronted mouth.

Nina stepped around him. He followed her down the hall, hissing at her like he always did.

Before she could make it back down the steps, he yanked her into her mother's bedroom. "I missed you," he said, locking the door behind him.

Nina remembered the many times he'd done this. The fear that he put in her that he would hurt her and her mother if she ever stopped his advances. Her mother was downstairs at the party, and she heard the loud music playing. This time, Mr. Darrell didn't scare her, and she was waiting for him to just get closer. Because she had something he wasn't expecting.

"C'mere," he said, roughly grabbing Nina by the waist. His hands felt down her ass. She backed him up closer to the desk where her mother kept her .38. He kissed her neck and bare shoulders. Nina closed her eyes and reached for the gun in the drawer without moving but an inch.

Just when Mr. Darrell was getting turned on, she kicked him between his legs until he fell back. When he lunged at her, she cocked the gun and he froze.

She slowly walked up to him, enjoying every step as she pressed the barrel of the gun in his neck. Every vision she'd had of him flashed before her, and she cocked it and let the cool steel rest against his skin. She didn't say a word, because Mr. Darrell's begging was all she wanted to hear.

"Do it, kill me, bitch, you probably couldn't if you tried," he said, laughing and crying at the same time.

"Let's see about that," Nina said, backed up, and shot a bullet into his chest, near his shoulder. Mr. Darrell fell back onto the bed. Nina dropped the gun and covered her mouth with her hands. She didn't know she could do it and she told herself if she'd done it years ago, maybe her life would have been drastically different.

Within moments, she heard several feet running up the steps. Nina's mother burst through the door with Trent. "Da hell?" Ms. Bettus asked as she looked at Mr. Darrell on the bed holding his chest, and at the blood-soaked sheets.

"You finally did it," Ms. Bettus said as she stood over Mr. Darrell, who was clearly in pain. But for once, he didn't matter. "If you couldn't kill me, you'd have to destroy me somehow."

"Mama, that man has destroyed me year after year since I was fifteen!" Nina yelled as she looked at Trent, who knew all about it. But he stared back at her in disbelief as if he was seeing an all-new person.

"I'm calling the police," Trent said, reaching for the phone, but Ms. Bettus stopped him. "No need to get the police involved; this is a family matter, woman to woman. Call the ambulance."

Nina was relieved; the last thing she needed was anything holding up her train to New York. She had to leave. Life here was not going to get any better. She didn't understand what she had done so wrong in her life to make her mother hate her. She had cursed about Nina to her aunt and uncles, and dragged her name through the mud.

Nina felt like she was about to have a nervous breakdown with what just happened. She broke out in a hot sweat all over and felt faint. She turned to leave.

"Wait a minute," Ms. Bettus said, holding Mr. Darrell in her arms, who was still alert but losing lots of blood. "I see you gonna make me choose between you and Mr. Darrell. Why don't you go back to your own husband and leave mine alone?"

"You already made your choice years ago," Nina spat back. "This is all your fault. If you would've stopped this monster or done something maybe this could've been avoided. You're lucky I didn't shoot him dead!"

"Get out of my house!" Ms. Bettus said, her eyes swollen with fury. "Before I have the police drag you out!"

Nina laughed to herself, and as she left, Trent and Ms. Bettus were hovering over Mr. Darrell. She knew deep down that her mother knew that this day had been coming. That was why she didn't call the cops; it was just the chickens coming home to roost.

four

Nina was feeling like a new woman. She had been in New York for only two weeks and four days, but already she felt stronger, and not a day older than her twenty-five years. Up until now, she had felt more like forty-five. The world looked friendlier, too. Dee hooked her up with a friend who owned a brownstone on Carlton Avenue in Brooklyn. The older lady, Ms. Bauer, was a single grandmamma type with gray hair, freckled light skin, and thick gray glasses. She agreed to rent Nina the first-floor studio apartment for half the rent. Ms. Bauer, who lived alone and had no children, hadn't rented out the apartment in years since she didn't trust people, but she trusted Dee. Nina was more than grateful for the modest apartment with a sleeping alcove, wood floors, and a nice bathroom on a tree-lined street. With what she had left over from Dee, Nina believed she had enough to hold her over until she started work. That was also falling into place. Just the other day, while window-shopping in Union Square in Manhattan, she had walked into a third-floor spa that was opening soon. It was called

Serenity. Nina told Delores, the owner, that she didn't have her certificate yet, but was well versed in most massage techniques that she had learned during her short time at the massage school in Houston. Delores had faith in Nina. Her desperate need for qualified massage therapists landed Nina the job right then.

The grand opening of Serenity would be in another week. Nina had some time to herself to explore her new surroundings. A few days prior, a petite, thin brother, with dreads down his back, had been standing in front of the Q train station giving out invitations for a poetry set. Nina didn't get a good look at him in the quick rush hour madness of Flatbush Avenue, but she took the card anyway. She also felt that he looked strangely familiar, like she had seen him around Houston, but she was sure she hadn't after she heard his name, "Ahmasi." No one she knew had a name she couldn't spell.

That same night equipped with a MetroCard and the postcard, Nina took the train to the city. She had never listened to poetry, but she thought it would be something to do instead of sitting home and hearing Ms. Bauer scold her cat upstairs. She thought it would also be nice to meet some black people her age, since most of her neighbors were young and white couples.

The Teacup Lounge was in a discreet location on Bethune Street. Having only been in New York City for a few weeks, Nina wasn't well versed in the twists and turns of the city. It was nothing like her small town near Houston where she'd go to the creek and spend a lazy Saturday eating pickles under the fountain or talking to Dee when Trent deemed it was "okay." Orange Creek was like her own little corner of the world. She'd just sit and lose herself among the guitar-toting or ball-juggling street performers who were mostly neighbors who had come out to try to keep things interesting. If only everything in life could be so simple, she thought as she walked up the block. After asking a few people on the quiet street, she spotted the place. Right underneath the bridge at Westbeth was a black steel door with some women wrapped in head scarves and dreadlocked men standing in the front.

Nina passed them. She was beginning to think she had overdressed in a yellow vintage summer dress, and her wedge-platformed sandals were beginning to bother her. The lady at the shop told her that it was what New York women dressed like in the summer, but it didn't look like it from the women she had seen. She walked into the dark club, went up to the cashier window, and showed her ID and postcard. "How much?" she asked.

The young woman with the close-cropped boy cut glanced at the postcard and said, "Oh, you're on Ahmasi's list. It's free, baby." She added with a coy grin, "Good luck."

Nina walked up the steep steps as she thought about what good luck the girl was referring to. She knew it didn't have anything to do with the show. But she didn't stay in that thought mode for long. She changed her suspicious demeanor to one that said she belonged here. She sat down at the bar, squeezing in between a group of women drinking a strange, thick, green concoction.

"I'll have a margarita," Nina said, loudly over the thumping jazz that played in the background. The bartender leaned in to get a better earshot.

"Margarita!" Nina said, but louder this time so the people around her turned around.

The bartender, a curly-haired Hispanic man with sleeves rolled up to his elbows, looked bored. "We don't serve alcohol. Can I get anything else for you?" he asked, his mouth trying its best to smile.

Nina looked around to see what everyone else was having. "Well, what do you serve besides juice and soda?"

"Juice and soda." The bartender appeared exhausted already with Nina's indecisiveness.

"I'll have what these girls next to me are having. It looks good."

"My pleasure," the bartender said. He pulled out a glass and poured the green mixture into it. Nina was starting to have second thoughts at the lumpy texture, but had always been careful about not getting anyone preparing her food or drink annoyed.

The bartender took a napkin and placed the tall, filled glass on top of it. "Nine dollars," he said, taking out his hand.

Nine dollars! Nina wanted to give the drink back, but it was too late. She had never paid that much for a drink. Back home, that would've been grocery money. It would also get her a dinner special with dessert back home. Nina reluctantly gave him the money and took a sip of the drink. She couldn't swallow what felt like wads of cotton being pushed down her throat. She sipped again and asked the women next to her, "What the hell is this?"

"The green smoothie," they all said in unison. A tall girl with a short, curly haircut said, "It's made with spirulina, wheat grass, and physillium husk. It's good for your brain cells and blood. If you sprinkle some lemon juice in it, it usually tastes better."

What the fuck? Nina thought to herself. Alcohol had always been good for her brain. She nearly threw up when she heard the word "husk." All she could think of was eating the bones of a dead elephant. Bringing her hand to her neck, Nina said, "Thank you," and walked away as calmly as she could. She had realized that this crowd was into a whole new mixture of things, and it wasn't just smoothies.

The lounge was nothing more than one large room, filled with a young black group of artsy caricatures sipping on health formulas and smoking weed. She thought about this contradiction and smiled to herself. Thank God, she thought, that she didn't know where the hell she was or she would have bolted already. Instead, she decided to relax and take it all in. As she bopped her head up and down to the jazz tune, she pretended to drink from her glass. She smiled at the people who were looking at her as her body swayed to the music. Just as she was getting into it, the music stopped.

"Peace and love," said a throaty voice that seemed to come out of the sky. Nina looked up onstage and saw the spotlight on the lonely mike stand. "We gonna open our show with the hottest poets in the New York City area before we bring on our headliner, Ahmasi, the Brother Wonder." The room broke out in applause, and Nina noticed one table that was louder than the others. Behind the flailing arms and head wraps sat a small guy with dreads bigger than he was, looking shy but handsome with dazzling dark eyes and smooth dark chocolate skin. It was Ahmasi, the guy with the postcards. Nina thought about approaching the table and saying "hi" but didn't in case he was seated with his girlfriend. She watched Ahmasi's interaction with the others at the table, all women. There was a lot of smiling going on and laughing, but he was mostly on the listening end. The women were flirtatious, stroking his arm, brushing their shoulders against his when they laughed, and touching his chin from time to time. Nina haunted the periphery for his attention, knowing sooner or later they'd bump into each other in the crowded place.

Nina sat down a few tables behind Ahmasi and tried to appear interested in what she thought was more rap than poetry performed by a young baseball cap–wearing brother. One of Ahmasi's female companions left the table to walk to the bathroom. Nina waited, and the woman passed her seat some minutes later.

Nina stood up. "Hi, excuse me, I'm Nina."

"Yeah?" asked the girl who was wrapped from head to toe in a green checkered garb.

Nina put down her drink. "Well, I just wanted to know if Ahmasi has gone on yet. I'm here to see his show."

The girl's expression relaxed. "Oh, sister, Ahmasi don't go on until later. He's the headliner, so you haven't missed a thang," she said, patting Nina's shoulder. "This is his second time here, and his poetry is strictly for the ladies."

"Really? I just heard about it through a postcard he gave me," Nina said, wanting to know more.

"My name is Sister Isis," she said, giving Nina's hand a firm shake. "Look, we have been trying to promote this event everywhere. As you can see, there is standing room only. It's great for you to join us!"

"No problem," Nina said, taken in by the girl's sudden friendliness. "I'm having a good time."

"Well, would you like to meet Ahmasi now? He's right over there chilling," Isis pointed out.

Nina thought there was no girlfriend at the table, but she wasn't sure about talking to him around his female entourage. "Oh, no, I can wait till later."

"Okay, but we'll talk." And with a wave of her hand, Isis walked back to Ahmasi's table.

Nina knew that chatty Isis would go back to the table and repeat their conversation, making Ahmasi notice. Nina wasn't the type to intrude on other people's territory and never thought going up to a man first was the thing to do. She had to be careful, she thought, she was a newbie in her new city and didn't know the angels from the devils. But Nina thought about Ahmasi and his poetry, about how every woman was probably like a piece of art to him. She imagined how nice it would be to be with a man who appreciated a woman for being a woman.

Peering over at Ahmasi's table, Nina saw Isis talking to him and him shaking his head agreeably. Then she pointed, and Ahmasi looked up in Nina's direction. Nina pretended to be distracted by looking for something in her purse. All of a sudden, she felt a shyness come on. What if they were talking about her? Bad things? she asked herself. That was how it usually was. People always had something to say. She was embarrassed that all eyes were on her. When she looked up, Ahmasi was standing there in blue jeans and a black and white T-shirt looking down at her.

"So what do you think about the Green Drink?" Ahmasi asked, his hands hiding in his pockets. Nina liked the way he smelled, like thyme. The smell reminded her of her mother's herb garden. But when she inhaled again, it smelled like women's perfume. It smelled very much like her own. Could he be wearing women's cologne?

Nina remained sitting and took a generous sip of the drink. "Oh, it's different. I haven't had one of these in a while," she heard herself lie. "I mean, I never had one of these before. I'm not even from around here." Nina thought that she didn't want to play the role like none of this was new to her. She wanted to be relaxed. She didn't want to keep anything bottled up inside of her like she had done for years. She was free now. And if he had a problem with that, Nina thought, it would be his problem all alone.

"Uhm, are you okay?" Ahmasi asked. "You look really distracted."

Nina snapped out of her mental rant. "I'm sorry," she said, touching her forehead, "I was just thinking to myself. I got a lot on my mind." Nina stirred her drink with a straw.

Ahmasi's eyes fell on Nina's yellow dress with green leaves embroidered on the edges that she had bought at a small vintage shop in Brooklyn. Her hair was neatly tied into a bun, and she wore a rich shade of red lipstick.

"Do all women from where you're from wear pretty yellow dresses?" he asked, his voice so low that Nina had to strain to hear it. "Can I sit down?"

"Sure," Nina said, feeling flattered and more comfortable with his presence.

"The bright yellow reminds me of the banana vendors in Kingston."

"Jamaica?" Nina asked, her lips poised at attention. Her eyes canvassed Ahmasi's neatly combed goatee and carved, high cheekbones that made his face look like an African warrior's.

"Yeah, Jamaica," Ahmasi answered. But Nina was anxious to find out more about Ahmasi's connection to the island. She had heard from Dee a while back that Jamaican men were some of the best lovers on the planet. Love was someone who hadn't lived in her home or even heart for years.

"Are you from there?"

"No, but everybody thinks I am. Where are you from?"

"Near Houston, just moved out here. I lived in a little town you probably never heard of."

"Hmm, I been to Houston. I may know—"

But as soon as she was about to tell him to elaborate, the music stopped again.

"Let's get ready for the real soul food. Our headliner tonight is straight outta Brooklyn, been holding his own in the underground for years . . . our man, Ahmasi—"

The light dimmed and the lounge quieted after a long round of applause. "Excuse me," Ahmasi said, rising gracefully from the table. "I'll only be a minute."

Nina smiled and looked on curiously as Ahmasi approached the stage with his hands folded behind his back and his head looking down. She was already feeling him.

The room was still except for a few whispers and clinking of glasses. Everyone had their eyes glued to the stage. Nina wanted to be the only lady he recited poetry to tonight. *Mmm. I am due some romance. And if I can get none, I might as well fake some.* Nina closed her eyes as she got ready to listen.

Ahmasi wetted his lips and began.

"Disgusting . . .
The things people call the things I envision
The spice that Marco Polo could not find on his trail
I'll find in your treasure trail from your navel to your stable
Melted kisses dissolve in you to make you cum to my side
Of the Jungle
Nina: a black bitch with a deadly switch
Lions lay at your feet to protect you from apes
That masturbate in the trees infected by an ass black as
Olives, thick as collards, I laugh at the knowledge
Telling me I'll never possess an ass round enough to start a war
Eyes with no reflection, heart with no affection,
discretion with no direction
Bitch, sin one more time so I can split you like dark oak,
with a mighty lumberjack stroke
Creamy thighs, juicy lips, and a conceited nose
Pussy tighter than calf muscles when standing on tippy toes
Laugh, pretty bitch, like I don't exist
I'll be the one to jump down on you in a heated fit."

The crowd broke out in applause. Nina almost suffocated. It wasn't that romantic at all, she thought. From the sounds of the poem, she believed that there was more to Ahmasi than that tender, sweet side he showed earlier. And she liked it. But she wondered if he was talking about her. He used her name. Eyes with no reflection? Discretion with no direction? She didn't know how he could size her up in such a brief meeting. Nina looked over at the table of girls he had been sitting with, and each one gave Nina a stiff, cold look. Nina was confused. She thought the poem was a diss, but everyone seemed to think it was a homage to her. She did like the part about the conceited nose. That was cute, she thought. She had never been the subject of anybody's anything, at least not in a good way. She caught Ahmasi's wink at her. Some people in the crowd smiled at her. Nina smiled, and then finally clapped. He read two other poems. Nina realized that he was making up the poems onstage right then and there. And she thought it was tight. Ahmasi could very well be gifted and not even know about it. By his last poem, he had the crowd on their feet like at a rap concert.

After Ahmasi was done with his set, Nina sauntered past the small crowd that had gathered by the stage and made her way over to him. He was looking over a stack of postcards with another gentleman.

"Were you trying to tell me something earlier?" Nina asked, smiling brightly, as he smiled back the same.

"Maybe I was saying something you already believed. It would only mean something if it applied to you," he said.

"Okay, none of that double-talk. I know you were trying to say something. But I will have you know that I do have direction," she said defensively. She wondered for a moment if she was just convincing herself and not him. "And it's pointing up, not down, if I have anything to do with it."

"Cool, not a problem," he said, swinging a few locks off his face. "You just seemed so timid and unsure of yourself earlier and now you seem so confident, like a different woman."

"I am every woman. Didn't you hear the song?" Nina laughed.

Ahmasi did, too. "Listen, I would never try to use a ploy to get a woman's attention. But if it worked, so be it."

"So be it," Nina said, tilting her head to the side as she met his eyes.

Ahmasi fiddled with the key chain that hung from his baggy jeans pocket. "Can I call you?"

Nina was glad he asked. He would be her first official New York friend. "I'll call *you*," Nina said.

Ahmasi pulled out a pen and brown leather notepad with engraved Chinese letters from his back pocket. "Here it is," he said, taking his time to neatly write down the long, thin strokes of numbers.

Nina folded the paper up and stuck it in her purse. "Thank you for inviting me tonight," she said, and hugged him. He felt like a sack of twigs to her. Light, but hard. She prayed that green drinks weren't the only thing in his diet. "I'll call you soon."

five

Serenity was finally open. Nina was two weeks into her job and enjoying the experience of being new to everything. Her new job even inspired her to learn as much as she could so she could open her own spa one day. With Dee's help, she was able to send Trent divorce papers. She hoped that he wouldn't take too long getting back to her. A small part of her wanted him to call and ask her why and fix it. She was used to depending on him and letting him call the shots. Though she knew it was best, she was scared. Scared that the divorce could get ugly, scared that the last five years had been a waste, and scared that it would be too long again before a man walked into her life. But she had never been a woman to sit around waiting for a man, and they came eventually, like buses, pulling up one by one, until she decided to get on.

For now, she was relieved to have a job where she could use and build on her skills. It gave her the confidence she had lost. It was a professional environment, where most of the services were therapeutic and clients were accident victims. Delores provided some specific training techniques of her own to the small staff. She wanted to make sure everyone understood the importance of drawing a line between the client and themselves. Delores was adamant about not forming any ties with any clients, and she never gave them the same client more than twice. Nina didn't understand what the big deal was. Most of the clients were old, married, or athletic-type women. Her first client was a seventy-six-year-old grandfather who slept during his Swedish massage. Nina had a headache after that treatment. She remembered having to put her finger under his nose at moments to make sure he was still breathing. Another client was a six-year-old boy who'd had a serious bike accident and needed a simple massage treatment to soothe his bruised muscles. Everyone was different and she took interest in their particular needs. She reveled in meeting new faces, and getting to know them, but she obeyed Delores's rules. Delores was a veteran in the business, and Nina respected her way of doing things.

"Hey, Nina, how you keeping up?" Melanie, one of Nina's colleagues, asked. Melanie was Puerto Rican and if it wasn't for her short, cropped hairdo, she could pass for Jennifer Lopez's twin.

"I'm doing okay," Nina said as she wrapped her mint-green uniform jacket around her. "I got a late client today."

"What time?" Melanie asked, taking hers off.

"Seven P.M." Nina looked in the mirror and applied some chocolate brown lip gloss to her succulent mouth, one of her best features.

"Girl, that is late. I will be on the train at that time. But I guess there will be days when I gotta work late, too."

"I don't mind. I live alone. Working late gives me something to do. Gets my mind off me, for a while."

"How's that divorce going?" Melanie asked.

"It's going. I'll give him another few weeks before I start catching a fit. If I have to bring his hand to the paper I will," Nina said, surprised by the tone of her voice.

"Is that right? With your little quiet self, I didn't know you had that side to you," Melanie said, looking at Nina dead-on.

"Well, I do have a little thug up in me." Nina laughed as she put her makeup supplies away.

"Do you want one?"

"Excuse me?" Nina asked.

"Maybe you need a *real* thug up in you. Help you get over all that drama. You can lay back and let him suck it all out of you," Melanie said with a sly look.

Nina looked over her shoulders at Melanie. The proposition wasn't so bad, she thought. She squeezed her thighs at the thought of some good lovin'. It didn't have to come with any strings; she had enough of that already. But she wasn't that cool with Melanie yet to ask for the hookup. She figured in time she'd get what she needed. "I think I'm all right for now," Nina said as she combed her hair and tucked the edges behind her ears. Her simple, straight cut looked neat and stylish.

"That's what we all say, until we break down and find ourselves with our three-hundred-pound neighbor on our hands and knees," Melanie said, like she knew all about it.

"You are a trip," Nina said, smiling. "I'll take my chances. But wait, aren't you married?"

"I am, but I'm seeing someone."

"The three-hundred-pound neighbor?" Nina giggled.

"No, but a 215-pound, six-foot-tall, dark Cuban import. I think I love him."

Nina caught Melanie's eyes and realized she was serious. "Why don't you tell your husband if it's like that? If you really love this man."

"Oh, please, girl. That is how you American women handle stuff. Tell your husband everything under the sun. It doesn't work. I like being married, but not to Pablo. He's such a motherfucker. I wish he would catch me fucking Javier so he could leave me. Believe me, I tried to get caught."

"I see," Nina said, not wanting to add her two cents yet. She didn't like telling married women what to do because she had seen it backfire so many times on friends. "Just be careful, whatever you do."

Melanie smiled at Nina. "I think you know where I'm coming from. And it's not gonna take you long before you meet somebody that will have you calling his name."

Nina smiled faintly at Melanie as she left. She thought Melanie was interesting and maybe somebody to get to know.

Moments later, Delores walked in. "Nina," she said, peeking through the door. "Sorry about this again. I'm still short-staffed. I promise I'll try not to book you for an hour and a half so late in the evening. I appreciate this."

Nina shrugged. "I'm fine, Delores. Anytime you need me, I'm here," she said as Delores stuck her pudgy, round body in the door.

"There's one thing, though. He's rather handsome. So be careful. We pride ourselves on our utmost professionalism. I trust you," Delores said, and closed the door.

Nina stared blankly at the closed door. She thought something awful must have happened to Delores to be so neurotic. Nina looked at her watch and realized it was that time. She walked to the waiting room for her client to introduce herself. When Nina got there, all she saw was a pair of big, broad shoulders clad in a white robe and a bald, black, shiny head. Since she started, Nina hadn't had a black client yet. But it had only been two weeks.

His back was facing her as he sipped on a glass of lemon

water. Nina tapped him gently on his shoulder. "Excuse me, Mr. Franklin?" she asked.

When he turned around, he flashed a dashing smile that lit up the room. "Yes, that's me."

"Hi, Mr. Franklin. I'm Nina, your massage therapist this evening," she said in an almost robotic way. But inside, she was moved by his masculine features—strong jaw, perfectly trimmed mustache that kissed his full, smooth lips, and deep-set eyes that seemed to hold the world and then some in them. If the outside looked that good, she had to wonder what the inside looked like.

"Follow me," Nina said as she walked beside him down the hall. She could feel Mr. Franklin's eyes checking her out. They walked by Delores's office, and Delores gave Nina a "remember what I said" look.

"Your name again?" Mr. Franklin asked as Nina closed the door behind him.

"It's Nina," she said, trying to avoid eye contact. She thanked God that he was a foot taller than her five-foot-three so they didn't have to meet eye to eye. "Is there any particular area you want me to pay extra attention to?"

"Don't you have my chart?" Mr. Franklin asked in a low, pleasant voice.

"Oh," Nina said, almost forgetting. The chart was on the table beside her. She was already showing signs of being distracted. *Focus, focus, focus,* she told herself.

Nina scanned the chart. "Okay, if you don't mind disrobing and lying down on the bed."

Mr. Franklin disrobed. He was wearing a pair of shorts, provided by the spa, that wasn't enough to hold in the bulging thigh muscles of his long, sculpted legs. Nina brought her eyes back to his chart. He was injured on a ski slope and had sore tendons. His procedure involved a whole Swedish body massage with special attention to his thighs.

"Are you comfortable?" Nina asked as she moved her eyes quickly off his speckled hair, his well-built chest. She dimmed the lights, a common practice for all clients of the spa. Delores thought it added to the mood of peace and serenity.

"Yes," Mr. Franklin said as he lay on his back.

Nina laid a dry, heated towel over the upper half of his body. Light classical music played in the background. The room was specifically set up for his preferences. Every client had a profile. Several candles were lit in the room, emanating the sweet, relaxing fragrance of lavender.

"I'm going to place a satin mask over your eyes. Is that okay?" Nina asked.

"Actually, I'll just keep my eyes closed if I can help myself." He smiled at her in a way that made her question what he meant.

Nina rubbed her hands with oils and began at his feet. She slipped her fingers into the crevices of his toes, massaging them with the tender care an artist would give to his painting. It also helped that his toes were well maintained and clean. All the while, Mr. Franklin's eyes were closed and he seemed entranced in his own paradise. Nina liked to see her clients relaxed, because it relaxed her, too. She moved her hands to his left leg and worked his thick calf muscles and dug her fingers into the grooves of his legs up to his thighs. He parted them slightly. She kneaded his thighs, massaging his tense muscles to a soft pulp. She was careful not to go anywhere near the inside of his mid-thigh. Delores always warned that men were extra sensitive even without direct contact with their private parts. Even a stray elbow or finger could trigger a standing ovation, and she wasn't talking about applause. Nina parted his legs some more to give her room. The warm, mahogany-coated skin of his thighs was smooth like satin with the subtle coarseness of hair. Her hands added more heat to his skin, and she marveled at its healthy condition. Being a therapist, she noticed these types of things. When she was done with both legs, she worked up to his chest and shoulders. Touching this man, she thought, was therapeutic for her, too. She missed touching and being touched. She liked the strength she felt in her hands as they moved over his body. She thought he would be the closest she'd get to a man like this for a while.

"Mr. Franklin," she whispered. "Please turn over," she said, applying some oil to her hands.

"Call me Lamont," he said, opening his eyes. She was glad he kept them closed because it would've freaked her out if she caught him staring.

"Okay, Lamont." She eyed his boxers and it seemed like he was more comfortable than she thought.

"Would you mind turning around for a second?" he asked bashfully.

"Oh, sure." Nina knew what was up, so to speak. She had to hold in her laugh, but wondered if she went wrong somewhere.

She waited until he turned around on his stomach and laid the towel across his upper half. If Lamont had a good front, his back certainly added to that. Nina rubbed more oil between her palms to get the heat going. She placed both hands on the back of his feet, moving up to the ankles, thighs, in slow, intense movements and pressure. His boxers hugged his tush to the point where she could see his shape. Delores definitely needed to order some specialized boxers for the brothers, Nina thought. His ass stood high on his back and was firm. She wanted to slap it to see if it bounced back. Delores could tell her where to touch, but she couldn't tell her what to think. Nina continued with the procedure until she was done. When it was through, she felt like she had just had good sex.

"Mr. Franklin, I mean, Lamont, you can come outside whenever you're ready," Nina said, turning up the lights slowly.

"Thank you," he said as he sat up. "That was the best massage I ever received."

"Oh, well, thank you. Glad you enjoyed it," Nina said as she nodded and walked to the door. "I'll meet you outside."

"Hold on, I wanted to know if I can, uhm, have lunch with you one day," he said, holding his hands up in a defensive way. "Just a simple lunch."

Nina felt that was coming. She closed the door. "We have a strict policy about dating our clients. I can't do that."

"It's not a date date. It's lunch. Or how about a phone call?" he suggested.

Nina liked his assertiveness and she kicked herself that those were the rules. "I'm sorry but I just started this job, and I like it. I don't want to cause any problems."

"Okay." He nodded as he folded his hands. He studied Nina's posture, which wasn't as confident as she sounded. She wanted to see him again. They both knew. "I respect that. Well, thank you again for the great massage."

Nina politely exited the room and exhaled. She waited outside for him as they were supposed to escort their clients out. Ten minutes later, he walked out of the room looking refreshed with a smile.

"Where do you live?" he asked.

"Brooklyn," Nina said quietly as they passed Delores's office.

"Interesting, I live there, too."

Nina paused at the reception desk. "Well, Mr. Franklin," she said, purposely calling him by his last name, "I am glad you enjoyed your experience. Please take care." Nina walked back to the office with her heart stuck in her throat. He was buttery fine, she thought. As she went back to the room to clean up, she still felt his energy there. The sheets smelled of sandalwood. The room was hot when they were both in there, but not anymore. She had never given a massage to anyone that she had had a connection with like that. It was definitely harder than anything she'd had to do since her New York arrival.

When she packed up for the evening, she checked her office box for her tips for the day. Everyone left something. The most she had ever gotten was twenty-five dollars. Delores let everyone keep their tips no matter how much they were. When she opened Lamont's envelope, it was thin. She figured she probably pissed him off at the end. But when she opened it she found a clean, crisp hundred-dollar bill. His procedure was less than that. He didn't leave a number or anything else, and, she thought, that was probably for the best.

six

A week later, Nina mustered up enough strength to call Ahmasi. She had never been good at dating because she had never really dated. She'd barely dated Trent because a month after the second meeting they'd had at her mama's house, he'd proposed. They had married three months later, but never had a honeymoon.

When Ahmasi picked up, Nina said, "Hi, remember me? It's Nina."

Ahmasi laughed right away. "I've been waiting for your call."

Nina figured Ahmasi could be a friend. She didn't know enough about him to say more right now, but she did have an attraction to him. She'd gotten a place, had a job, and now she wanted to have some fun. "What are you doing tonight?"

"Whatever you want to do."

"I don't know what to do. I've been in bed all day," she said, checking out the 9 P.M. time on the clock. There was an excitement for something new and different burgeoning up inside her. She was game for anything. "My landlady must think I'm a hermit. I haven't gone anywhere exciting since I moved here."

"I'm on duty. Can you be ready in an hour?" he asked.

"Sure, where are we going?" she asked, jumping out of bed and standing by the window. She gazed at the moon.

"Someplace you probably never been to, but wanted to. What's your address?"

Nina gave him the address and hung up. She didn't know what he meant, but she liked the suspense.

She quickly showered, threw on a black sweater dress, black shiny belt, and black knee-high boots. She wetted her air with a spray and scrunched it together for a nice wavy look. She was feeling great as she checked out her goods in the mirror. She wished Trent could eat his heart out now.

Nina walked over to the ringing phone. "Hello," she said, clipping on a pair of gold hoop earrings.

"Hello," Trent said dryly.

Nina nearly dropped the phone out of her hand. She had no idea how he got the number; Dee must've given it to him for some reason. But she wasn't mad. "When can I have the papers back?"

"I'm waiting on my lawyer to get back to me—"

"Trent, don't play games with me on this. I want those papers sent to my lawyer before the end of next week—"

"Or what?"

"Or—" She didn't know what to say. She squeezed the phone tightly in her hands. "Or I will get every dime you owe me. I'm giving you a clean slate right now, because I don't want any drama holding up my life."

"You got a life now?" he snickered.

"Whatever, Trent. You never really got to know who I really am as a woman."

"I know you almost killed Mr. Darrell. That's all I needed to know how much of a wretch you are."

"Trent, you cannot intimidate me with your words. Do what you gotta do, but you better get those papers back to me," Nina said, maintaining her cool as she got her purse together. "When I get them, I'll have my lawyer call your lawyer."

"Wait—" Trent said, before she hung up.

"What is it?" she asked, getting irritated at his arrogant tone.

"Listen, I still love you. Can we at least work this out? I need you."

"You need me because you know ain't nobody else cooking for no thirty church folk every week. You need me to be your maid, dishwasher, tailor, and nurse. But I got me somebody who's doing all that for me and more."

"You do?" he asked, distress all over his voice.

"Yes, and he's the best thing that's ever happened." She thought she had to lie to get him to realize it was over. Trent was as hard-headed as they came, and he only understood things in black and white. She had to make it clear for her own sanity.

"Fine, I bet that's why you moved, right? You had this all planned."

Nina didn't answer.

"You think you in this pretty little safe world right now, but wait and see. You still a backward-ass country girl. Just watch your back," he said, and hung up.

Damn. Nina hoped she hadn't made things more complicated. But she knew Trent would keep stringing her along if she didn't make it clear. She was also aware that his bark hurt more than his bite. She put the phone back on the charger, and began applying her mascara. Then the bell rang.

Nina headed quickly out the door.

"This cool with you?" Ahmasi asked, looking at her dress as she walked. He was sitting proud on a black, sleek motorcycle. "I hope you can ride in that."

"Definitely." Nina hiked up her dress to her thighs. Her coat and tall boots provided the warmth she needed. She hopped on the back of the bike, never having ridden on one in her life. She felt bad, she felt free. She zoomed away with Ahmasi, and as he sped off, Ms. Bauer peeked out of the top-floor bedroom.

A half hour later, Ahmasi pulled into a parking lot in Harlem that was jammed with everything from the latest Benzes to the oldest Camrys. There were several men and couples walking into the venue.

Ahmasi snatched off his helmet and let Nina remove hers. He ran his fingers through his wiry locks. "I hope you like strip clubs," he said as he gave her a random kiss on the cheek.

Nina liked the rough, edgy feeling of his locks against her face. "Uhm, I never been to one, but as long as you don't plan on leaving me alone in there, I'll be cool," she said, not wanting to sound boring. She thought, perhaps, this is what people did in New York.

"Cool," Ahmasi said as he stroked her face. "And it ain't your daddy's strip club. Everybody goes to the strip club because that's where the real party is these days. Haven't you seen all those rap videos?"

"Yeah, but that's fake."

"Hell no, it's real. The strip club is the new party club. Plain and simple. But if you feel uncomfortable at any time, we can bounce."

"I'm okay," Nina assured him, and appreciated his attentiveness.

He took her hand as they pulled up to the club door. The bright lights of the club highlighted its name—Take Two. There were no windows, a perfect escape.

There were several other couples going in and Nina felt completely comfortable, but she still kept a tight grip on Ahmasi's hand. When they got inside, the doorman asked Ahmasi, "Here for your weekly dose?"

Nina grinned at Ahmasi, who looked a little off guard. *Weekly,* she thought. He just didn't seem like the type; maybe that was why she felt so safe with him. He intrigued her even more than when they first met.

They checked their coats and took a seat at the bar. Ahmasi ordered the drinks. He knew the bartender by name: "Jewel." The club smelled like smoke, sweat, and sex running through the stale air. Two girls swiveled their hips on stage as flurries of singles gathered at their feet. In the corner, covered by the shadow of the stage, was a thin Hispanic girl letting a man squeeze her breasts.

Nina casually sipped her rum and Coke and soaked it all in. She wasn't embarrassed because she didn't know anyone. She wasn't afraid that anyone would recognize her. She felt like she was watching a movie, waiting to see what was going to happen next. She decided to sit back and chill as Ahmasi's attention was drawn to "Candy," a thick, chocolate-brown girl with wide hips, a tiny waist, and long, curly hair. Nina was fascinated by how women like these did it. A small piece of crimson see-through material covered her breasts and bottom. A thin, dark strip of hair between her legs showed through. Nina felt awkward looking at the girl, but after several more sips of her drink, she felt herself turned on by the sexual energy charging through the air. The girl stripped down. Then she gave one man a lap dance. And then another. And another. She moved her body like a snake, bouncing in all the right places. She crawled up to one guy who was throwing five-dollar bills at her. Her tongue traced the top of his forehead and went down to his chin. He reached in his pocket and stuffed a twenty-dollar bill in her ass crack as she danced on him. Then he slid a ten between her lips. She stood up and wiggled her ass before his face. He slapped it and she shook it even harder. The red strobe light reflected the beads of sweat rolling down her back. Ahmasi was spellbound. As for Nina, she had counted that the girl must have collected over a hundred dollars for a twenty-minute performance.

Jewel handed them two more drinks. These were on the house. Candy came toward them, rolling those hips in front of Nina, but Nina pointed to Ahmasi. Candy sat on the bar and pressed her chest up against him, her titties hitting him in the chin. Nina cracked up a bit as his mouth tried to follow her motions. Then Candy dropped on his lap. She rode him slow and deliberately. Not hard and fast like she did the other guys. Nina realized why he was a regular at this joint.

The girl did most of the work, as Ahmasi sat still. Then she whispered in his ear, "Hit the drum, baby."

Ahmasi tapped her round bottom and cupped the cheek tightly between his hands. Nina got in a few slaps, too. She was having fun, and couldn't help herself. Candy picked up her pace as more sweat drizzled down her cleavage. Candy and Nina seemed to be getting more out of it than Ahmasi. When she felt her tips dry up, Candy hopped back on the bar and jiggled away. Nina's eyes followed her. Then she turned to Ahmasi. She put her hand on his dick.

"You're not hard," she said, surprised as hell.

"I don't get hard off of that. I need romance. You know, like a woman does." He laughed as he wet his lips with the drink. "Can we get romantic?"

◆ ◆ ◆

Ahmasi opened the door to his place and let Nina in first. She grabbed a handful of Sun Chips from an opened bag on a table and flung herself on the sofa in the living room.

Ahmasi eyed her black boots.

"Do I need to take anything off?" Nina asked, feeling woozy from her several drinks.

Ahmasi sat next to her and reached for her left boot and gently tugged on it.

Nina looked up at him and smirked. She kicked out her right leg, and Ahmasi slid off her boot.

"Yeah, and these, too," he said, referring to her stockings. He slipped his hands up her dress so quick that Nina didn't have time to react, and slid the stockings down just as smooth. He held her right foot in his hand and placed his mouth on her covered toes.

"Ooh," she yelped. "Not the feet. That's my hot spot."

He tugged on her stocking foot with his teeth, never taking his hands off her. Nina's legs were bent at the knees and opened right in Ahmasi's face. She thought he was quite bold this evening and wondered what other things he might have planned. A drowsy feeling was settling on her that she fought off as best she could. He pulled her closer to him, and she let herself go with the flow. She admired the sexy, wild look of his black, shiny locks and dark, soulful eyes that drank her in. He kissed the big toe of both of her feet. She couldn't remember what condition her toes were in, but whatever it was, it pleased her that Ahmasi didn't give a damn.

He placed two more full-lipped kisses on her toes. "Now don't think I'm going to do this every time you walk in here with shoes," he said, now close enough that she could smell his Poison perfume. But he didn't get too close.

"Want something to drink?" he abruptly asked as he got up and walked to the kitchen. He peeked around the corner. "I would give you some coffee to shake off some of those drinks, but all I have is grape soda."

"Got any tea?"

"Yeah, I can do that."

"Good, with lots of sugar please." Nina sat on the floor where she was more comfortable. She wanted more of his foot kisses.

Ahmasi heated up some water in the microwave and walked back out in the living room with two steaming cups of tea. He sat on the couch and patted the space next to him.

Nina climbed on top of him. He wasn't exactly the thug type that Melanie may have suggested, but Nina thought he was good enough. And there was something rough about him, but she couldn't put her finger on it. She ran her fingers over his woolly but soft almond-scented locks, kissing the gentle slope from his nose to the curve of his lips. They both closed their eyes as their lips delicately touched again and again. Ahmasi's thumb grazed her nipples outside her clothes and he made little circles around her ears with his tongue. Nina loved that, a perpetual weak zone of hers. Then he whispered in her ear, "I know I may seem sweet, but I got a dark side to me, Nina."

Nina grinned. "Are you trying to turn me off or on?" What she really wanted was for him to keep quiet, so she could let off some of the stress on his body.

Ahmasi made a small laugh as he wrapped his hands around her waist. "I wanna taste the inside of you," he said, motioning for Nina to take off her clothes.

They both did. Ahmasi helped Nina with her white, sheer panties, slipping them off with his teeth. Nina lay on her back feeling like she was suspended in midair. It had been months since she had some downtown love. Trent had stopped doing that when he opened his "ministry." Ahmasi licked and sucked the edges of

Nina's shoulders to the tips of her nipples and the slope of her fleshy stomach. She relaxed her body as she let Ahmasi's tongue travel over her curves. The only thing she could hear was their panting in the dimly lit room. Then Ahmasi leaned over and sipped from his warm tea.

Nina figured maybe all that licking made him thirsty, but Ahmasi had a trick up his sleeve. He took a few quick drags from the hot tea and held the liquid in his mouth to get it nice and warm. He got down on the floor, spread Nina's pussy with his fingers, and covered it with his tea-warmed mouth. Nina gasped as the soft warmth of his mouth made her melt. She dangled her legs around his neck as he ate her like she was tonight's chef's special. His locks covered his face; only the pink of his lips and tongue were visible. As she caught her breath, he sipped some more of the tea, and did the same thing to get his mouth hot and soft. Nina had never experienced this before, but it was definitely creative. Ahmasi was on all fours as he teased her, moving his tongue lightly up and down, left to right, following her every move.

He inhaled the natural scent between her legs and it drew him in even more. He rose on top of her, slipped on a condom, and slid inside her slowly with care, as if she were made of pure crystal. As they rocked back and forth, Nina wrapped her legs around his waist and held her feet.

Ahmasi pushed deeper with a slow grind to his hips. He looked into her half-closed eyes, but Nina shut them. Their hips bopped together as she hung on to his shoulders. When he veered to the right, she did, too. "I think I love you," he moaned.

Nina pretended like she didn't hear that, but his lengthy dick reached a pleasure spot that made her eyes flash open. With her trembling thighs, she gripped his slippery back and said, "Thank you."

seven

Nina had known Ahmasi for only two weeks when they slept together. She had never bedded any man that fast before. The last man she bedded that fast, she married. There was just something about being in a place where nobody knew her name. She thought about how she could reinvent herself, and no one would know the difference. No one to judge her but herself. What surprised her more was that she felt guilty about not telling Ahmasi that she was going through a divorce. She didn't think it would've made a difference until they had sex. And she didn't see it as a onetime event either; she'd do it again. What she didn't see was a real relationship. She liked tall, masculine men, and Ahmasi was neither, but he was nice to her and good in bed. What she needed was to get her life back on track, and she wanted a man who had his head together already. She wanted a man who was stable and could take care of her. She wanted a man who could make her feel special and she didn't want to worry about keeping or getting a job. And no one was hiring poets the last time she checked.

On Monday, a few nights after their evening together, Ahmasi invited Nina to the lounge for his weekly poetry reading. She was off work and thought it would be nice to go back, as long as she didn't order the green juice.

They hung out at his table with Isis and Sura, who had aligned themselves as Ahmasi's unofficial fan club. There weren't as many women at the table as last time, and Nina was happy about that. Their table was situated at the far corner of the club, and every so often a person would pass by and give Ahmasi greetings or shake his hand. He was like a celebrity in his own little world.

Isis chewed on her tofu and sprouts pita sandwich as she listened intently to what Sura was saying about the struggle of today's artists. She was decked out head to toe in a matching blue and green head wrap and dress. Nina thought she had lots of style and looked like an African queen with her purplish black skin and light brown eyes. Once again, Nina felt she stood out with her straight relaxed hair, coochie cutter jeans, and black lace top.

"And I believe that once art becomes a vehicle for mass consumption, it will be eaten alive until all individuality is diminished," Isis said, as if this was an all-too-familiar topic. "Ain't that right, Ahmasi?"

Ahmasi and Sura nodded, but Nina just looked at Isis. She didn't know what mass consumption she was talking about. This wasn't exactly a conversation she had every day back home.

"Nina, Ahmasi is a real brother. He knows the true essence of the struggle of racism, sexism, and all the isms that have held our people back," Sura said as she dabbed the corners of her lipstick-free, natural mouth.

"Well, we always need more people, especially men, talking about what's important," Nina said as Ahmasi's grip around her waist got firmer. She reached for a French fry, the only thing on the menu she could eat.

"Girl, did he tell you about the time this guy stole his poem?" Isis said, leaning across the table.

The seriousness on her face alerted her. She wanted to know. "No, what happened?"

Isis pushed her finished plate away. "One night, Ahmasi was about to get onstage, but there was another poet named RonRon on before him. Anyway, come to find our ole boy gets onstage and says the poem Ahmasi was about to say. Ahmasi did his thing anyway, came up with a whole new poem off the top of his head, and he beat RonRon's ass down that night."

Sura added, "Come to think of it, no one has seen RonRon since then. Everybody says he's too embarrassed."

"Ahmasi fucked him up so bad, RonRon was in the hospital for a month with all kinds of—"

"Chill," Ahmasi said to them as he smiled awkwardly at Nina.

Nina didn't know what to think because she didn't know that Ahmasi could be that violent. *All over a poem?* Nina thought that was a little drastic. "Wouldn't you say that was overreacting a bit?" Nina asked Ahmasi.

Everyone looked at Nina like she had crossed into some unspoken territory.

Isis raised her finger in the air as she spoke. "A poet's poems are his lifeline. It is the blood he bleeds, and the air he breathes."

Nina chuckled to herself. "I haven't heard Ahmasi talk about poetry like that. That kind of talk takes the beauty out of it. It makes it like any other job."

Isis and Sura hissed like they didn't have time to educate Nina on the life of an artist.

"A man's soul is his most precious commodity. Poetry is the soul," Sura said calmly.

Nina rolled her eyes at them. They were taking this all too seriously, she thought. All the while, Ahmasi hadn't said a word. She wanted to know more about RonRon.

"So, do you go around putting people in the hospital?" Nina asked Ahmasi as Sura and Isis got up from the table.

"Nah," Ahmasi said with a grin. "That was just a necessary thing, but I do what I gotta do. Don't let the poems fool you."

Nina smiled.

"Let's go backstage so we can talk in private," he said.

Ahmasi and Nina relaxed backstage in a private room that was simply decorated with exotic gold and copper throws over the walls and chairs. "Are they always that serious?" Nina asked.

"Yeah," Ahmasi said as he rolled his dreads up into a crown on top of his head. "But it's probably the lack of vitamin E that got them so cranky tonight. They really cool." Ahmasi sat down across from Nina in another chair.

"Vitamin E?"

"They're dykes," he said and lit a joint. He passed it to Nina, who refused. She was ready for new things, but not that.

"It figures," she said, watching him as he smoked. She didn't like it, but it was what he was into. She was in no mood to change anybody.

Ahmasi, clad in black jeans and powder blue Tims that matched his shirt, swung his chair around. "So you never smoked?"

"Never," Nina said, crossing her legs. "I don't like the smell."

"But you'll love the feeling. You from Houston, right?"

"Yeah?"

"They smoke mad weed down there."

"How do you know?"

"I told you, I been there before."

"Where, exactly?"

"Where you from?"

"Allswell."

Ahmasi swiveled his chair around as he thought. *Allswell, Allswell.*

"Please, don't even act like you may know. It's a very small town."

"Yeah, it got that spot named Jake's Diner with a yellow awning?"

Nina laughed. "What da hell you doing in Allswell?"

Ahmasi laughed, too. "It may be small, but they got good weed."

Nina shook her head. There was lots of weed where she was from, and it was one of the few extracurricular activities for the people who lived there, besides making babies. But Nina was confused as to what Ahmasi had been doing there. She tried to think if she ever saw him because his look would've made him stand out. No one had dreads in Allswell.

"How long ago was it?" she asked.

"Maybe a few years. I had a little weed hustle going around. Know what I mean?" He grinned again. "Some people owed me some money, so I had to take a trip."

Nina was afraid to ask any more, but she made a note to ask Dee, who knew it all.

Ahmasi put the blunt between his lips, half closed his eyes, and emanated perfectly round smoke circles from his mouth. "Sure you don't want any?"

Nina shook her head.

"So tell me more about you. Why all the questions about me?"

Nina waved some of the pot smoke from between them. "What do you want to know?" Nina knew she had to tell him at some point about Trent.

"Is everything cool between us?" he asked.

"Why wouldn't it be?"

"I think I may have said something I shouldn't have the other night," he said with half a smile.

Nina shrugged, recalling his "I love you" comment. "I forgot about it. What was it?"

"Nothing," he said as he smiled and held his blunt away so the smoke wouldn't infiltrate between them. He stuck his chest out and said, "It's easy for me to fall in love with someone like you."

"Thank you," Nina said as she looked over his shoulders at her image in the mirror.

Ahmasi smiled some more. "I think I heard that before," he said. "What else should I know about you, Ms. Nina?"

He kept probing her, like he knew the answers. "I'm going through a divorce," she said. "I was married for five years, no kids."

"That's cool. As long as you divorcing the dude, and not marrying him, it's all good. Plus, you look like you running away from something. I could tell the first time I met you."

"Wow," Nina said, amused by how good he could read people because he was on point.

"I'm here for you, as a friend, if that's all you want."

"Thank—"

"Please," he said, almost about to laugh. "You've thanked me enough, for real."

They both cracked up. "You know what?" Nina said. "Let's just keep this simple. Whatever happens, happens."

"Cool."

The announcer called Ahmasi to the stage. Nina followed him and waited on the sidelines. She listened to every word of his performance. Like the audience, she was caught up. He was a small man in height, but he was big in every other way. He had a quiet swagger to him that made him taller than any tall man in the room.

Nina got to work a half-hour early the next morning. Unlike most people, who arrived to work late after a night out, she did what she had to do to arrive early. She needed the extra time to get her bearings after a heated night in bed with Ahmasi.

"Good morning, *chica,*" Melanie sang as she walked into the dressing room with a lively gait.

"Morning," Nina mumbled as she pulled her hair back in a ponytail and threw on her uniform. Her first client was due in twenty minutes.

"You okay?" Melanie asked as she opened her locker.

Looking in the mirror, Nina applied some mascara to her lashes and said, "Yeah, I just had a long night."

"How *long* was it?" Melanie flashed a look at Nina that indicated time wasn't what she was talking about.

Nina decided to have some fun with it. "Very, very long."

Melanie rushed over to Nina's side and emptied her makeup kit on the counter. "How long?"

"About thirteen inches. I swear." Nina was telling no lie as she smiled at Melanie's awed expression.

"I would be soaking in a baking soda bath right now!" Melanie shouted as she grabbed a tube of lipstick out of its case and spread the red color over her lips.

"Well, I'm getting used to it." And she was; Trent was average.

"So who is this guy?"

"He's someone I met just hanging out. He's a poet and he's nice to me." Nina didn't mind talking to Melanie. She thought that Melanie had problems with her husband, and they could relate. She didn't have to worry about being judged. And she needed a friend.

"You got a man already, and you barely been here a month," Melanie said, smiling brightly.

"He's just a friend. And he's not much my type. I like bigger guys."

"Bigger than thirteen?"

Nina laughed. "No, more masculine with muscles and all that. He's kind of petite. But I can work with it for now."

"I know you must get tired of sucking on that thing? If you wanna deep throat it, you have to—"

"Melanie, you are just *naaaasty*," Nina teased. "I haven't gone down on him. Sucking on him would be like sucking on a tuba."

"You need any help?" Melanie asked, winking at her.

They busted out in laughter. Nina thought Melanie was hilarious and reminded her of Dee.

Then Delores opened the door. "Nina, can I speak with you for a moment?"

Nina followed Delores down the hall and closed the office door behind her.

Delores sat down at her desk, her red face puckered up in deep contemplation. "So, I have a question for you."

Nina gave Delores her undivided attention. "I'm all ears."

"Well, it seems like this Mr. Franklin liked our services so much he wants to come back."

"Great." Nina always liked her clients to have a good experience.

"But he's asked only for you. Do you know why?"

Nina looked around the room as if the answer were written on the wall. "I don't, but isn't it a good thing?"

"Oh, it is, but I told him you were booked, and he didn't want to see anyone else."

"I see."

"And I just think that there could be more between you. He's a very handsome, robust man. You know our policy."

"Delores, uhm, I don't even know Mr. Franklin. Maybe he just liked how I did my job."

"Nina," Delores said, like she was talking to her own child. She tapped the edge of her pencil on the desk as she paused. "The reason why I have a policy that no therapist see a client more than twice is because of this."

"But I saw him once."

"Yes, and before it happens again, I wanted to talk." Delores managed a warm smile. "We also want to protect our therapists as some clients can get too attached. Also, if a relationship doesn't work out, I don't want to lose clients. You are all very attractive men and women in a very intimate position with strangers. We don't want to run this like a dating service."

Nina nodded.

"I have Mr. Franklin booked for you on Thursday afternoon at 6 P.M." Delores checked off something in her notepad. "Okay?"

"Sure," Nina said as her heart did a pitter-patter move. Delores looked too concerned, and she didn't want to risk her job. Losing her job would make her lose her direction. She had a plan. She needed this job.

"Great," Delores said.

Nina walked out of the office and prepared for her next client, a thirty-five-year-old woman who was coming for basic massage.

What does that man want? Nina thought to herself as she prepared the massage room for her appointment who was already ten minutes late. Mr. Franklin was as fine as can be, but she remembered being very clear with him that she couldn't date clients. She didn't want to cancel his appointment with her, but she wished she could. Somehow, she thought, he was going to get his way.

eight

Trent never agreed with many of Nina's ideas and the divorce was something he didn't see coming. He had to give her credit. But New York, out of all places, wasn't where he expected he needed to go. He had some dirty laundry down there, but for Nina's sake he hoped it didn't catch up with her. But if it did, so be it, Trent thought. When she found the papers in his drawer, he almost let the truth out right then and there. That was too high a price to pay.

"When is she coming back?" Rebecca asked as she lay in bed with Trent on Tuesday morning. Rebecca, a thirty-three-year-old white woman with loads of cash, owned a slew of fancy homes from Dallas to Houston. It was with her money and good credit that Trent was able to buy the numerous homes he rented out.

"Not sure," Trent answered as Rebecca nibbled on his soft, hairy chest covered in gray hairs. He didn't want to tell her about the divorce yet, because she'd get too happy and want him to commit to her. "She said she'd be gone for a few months."

"Are you getting a divorce?"

"I don't know."

"I'll get you the best lawyer—"

"I'm fine, Rebecca. She found out about the money and went away to get her mind straight."

Rebecca flipped her long, fiery red hair to her side. Her hair grazed Trent's skin as she raised her body over him.

"You mean she found out about *my* money."

"Right," he said, his hands running down her back. Rebecca was a workout maniac, but managed to keep all her curves. Trent loved to tease her and call her Tina Marie, because she was one white woman with a black woman's edge.

"Talking about my money. I'm sure she went to New York with some of it."

"I don't know whose money she used, but it ain't yours or mine," Trent said as Rebecca rolled off him.

"What do you mean?" she asked.

"I said, I don't know!"

"Don't get all siddity with me. I deserve to know what happens to every penny I give you."

"Well, don't worry, I plan to pay you back every dime."

"I won't hold my breath, baby. I've lost count already."

Trent ignored her. He hated when she acted this way. This was the only way she could control him.

"Did you hear me?" she asked.

"Yes, baby, I heard you."

Rebecca slid over to her side of the bed and rested her head on her hand. "I don't like being mean to you, honey. I just can't keep doing this."

"Listen, I just need you to do me one favor, that's all."

"What?"

"I owe somebody twenty thousand dollars. This cat in New York and—"

"Are you sending that bitch money!?" Rebecca fired off.

"No, not at all. I mean, I want a clean slate with this dude. And I need you to lend me the money."

"What's it about?"

"You know, I can't get into that," Trent said, peeking out the window to eye the black Benz she bought him for his birthday. His plan was to get the money from Rebecca, give it to his boy, then dump her. He was tired of her. But not until he sucked the last drop.

Rebecca climbed out of her bed and covered her naked body with a black cashmere robe. She peered out the window of the master bedroom of her six-bedroom mansion in the exclusive section of Houston. She didn't want to be in this situation. But when Trent put the moves on her two years ago at a neighborhood pool hall she owned in the downtown area, she couldn't resist. If lending him the money was what he needed, then she wouldn't do anything less.

Trent knew that Rebecca was getting too attached and he wanted to keep their relationship under wraps. It wouldn't look good on him, especially with the divorce with Nina getting around. He had a reputation he had to protect.

"I'll have the money transferred to your account in the morning," Rebecca said, feeling weary about it all.

"Cool," Trent said, as he had already mustered up a plan on how he was gonna spend it. He didn't plan on paying his friend back just yet. "Come here, girl," he said, pulling her back to the bed, as he lodged kisses on her large, pink breasts.

As he and Rebecca rocked back and forth on her imported

Egyptian cotton sheets, he realized that the only person he had to look out for now was himself.

In the morning, Trent delivered the divorce papers to his attorney. He also received the money from Rebecca as she'd promised. He lined up his ducks. His attorney assured him that his assets were protected and that the money Rebecca gave him was his to keep because they were "gifts." He was coasting. His next move may even be a trip to Monte Carlo, he thought to himself as he left his lawyer's office. But there was one thing.

Trent called Nina as he cruised in his Benz. "How's my ex-wife?" he said as she picked up the phone.

"Better now that you gave in on those papers. You did, right?" she asked.

"Sure did," he said, rolling up the windows so he could hear better. "But let me tell you something before you hang up—"

"Make it quick," Nina demanded. "Unlike some people, I work."

"Good for you. But I want to have you know that I was the best thing you ever had. The next Negro is gonna have some big ass drawers to fill."

"Big ass is exactly right," Nina said.

Trent huffed. He secured his earpiece in his ear. "You think everything is so good now. But you in New York, so you better watch where you laying your head at night."

"What you mean?" Nina asked, now concerned.

"I heard you seeing somebody named Ahmasi."

"How the hell you know?"

"That Ms. Bauer is one nosy old bitch, that's how I know."

"But you don't know Ms. Bauer."

Trent loved the shaky, shocked voice that Nina had. Gone was her overconfidence.

"Seems like one night when he picked you up, the old lady peeped it and called Dee. Just so happened that I overheard Dee talking at the bank about some motorcycle you was on before she left to Detroit."

"And?" Nina asked.

"And I know that nigga. He's a fucking weed hustler and I owe him some money—"

"Trent, I don't want to be in any dirty business of yours."

"You already in it. Just tell the nigga that I got his money." With that, he disconnected the call and smiled, knowing that he'd really fucked Nina's head up.

nine

At work, Nina replayed her conversation with Trent over and over. She called Dee's phone several times, but there was no answer. She called her house and her husband said she was still in Detroit at a business conference. She wasn't mad at Dee because she'd always known she had a big mouth, but she needed some advice. She had forgotten that Ahmasi had his name on his plates and that was what Ms. Bauer must have read that night, or it could be that Ms. Bauer was eavesdropping on her. Her mind was racked with all kinds of ideas. She wasn't ready to talk to Ahmasi yet, because she had an important client she had to see.

"Good to see you again, Mr. Franklin. Follow me, please," Nina said, trying to put her focus back on her job. She was doing her best to be as reserved as possible. He looked as delicious as he had during their first meeting, wearing a dark gray suit with a black Yves Saint Laurent embroidered tie.

"Here you go, Mr. Franklin. I'm just gonna give you a few minutes, and I'll be back." Nina escorted him into the room.

Mr. Franklin put his briefcase down and loosened his tie. "It's okay if you call me Lamont. I hope I didn't get you in any trouble."

"Not at all, Mr. Franklin. I'll be back in a few." Nina closed the door behind her and took a deep breath. Her skin smelled of him, and they hadn't even touched yet. A soothing, vanilla sandalwood scent infiltrated her nose and made her wonder what he bathed in to smell so good. He was a man, she thought, who treated himself well. A man who treated himself well physically and emotionally will treat his woman even better. At least, that was what she had been told by her father long ago.

When she returned to the room, he was lying on his back under the warm sheets. Nina dimmed the lights and played the classical music he asked for on his preferences sheet. She poured orange-scented oil on her palms and began to massage him like she did before. Beginning at his feet, she let her mind wander to all the bills she had to pay. She thought about anything that wasn't about his gorgeously sculpted body, his dimpled broad shoulders, and his thick, solid ass.

Lamont turned over for the second half of his massage. His face flushed with red. "Sorry," he said.

Nina huffed, "It's okay," a little annoyed that he was hard again. She understood that it happened with male clients, but the fact that she liked him, too, made it extremely uncomfortable. She wasn't offended, though, and wanted to see more. She wanted that towel to fall off so she could get it over with. She would have seen his dick and that would be that. There couldn't possibly be any other way to get closer.

She worked her hands over his shoulders, kneading them to complete his surrender to her power. Her fingers tingled with each touch against his oiled, slicked, dark brown skin. He didn't say a word, but inhaled deep and solid breaths. They both were silent, careful not to say anything that would lead to something more.

Forty-five minutes later, Nina twisted the caps back on the bottles of oils and situated Mr. Franklin's restful body. "That's all for today. When you're ready—"

"I'm ready now," Lamont said as his eyes enveloped her. "Can we *please* go on a date?"

Nina turned around and studied his handsome, quizzical expression. "Mr. Franklin, we can't date our clients. That's final."

"Can you think about it?"

Nina couldn't believe how determined he was. As much as she liked him, she liked her job better. One thing would definitely shut him down, she thought. "I'm going through a divorce now," she revealed.

"Oh." Lamont frowned and looked at her hand, which was absent of its ring.

Nina stood her ground.

"I don't care," he said as he gently took her hands. "Let me help you get your mind off some things. Just a date, please."

Nina felt her body simmer in his hold. She was close enough to kiss, but she wasn't moving. She didn't want him to let go for a second. She would love to go out with him under any other circumstances, but she also knew if she said no, he would only call for another appointment. At least this way, if it all went well, she could give him personal massages at home.

"If we go out," Nina began, her chest pressed against his, "I have to be very discreet about it. Plus, you can't ever call here for me."

"Deal."

• • •

Melanie invited Nina out after work to a lounge called Wish, a local spot that sold five-dollar margaritas and twenty-five-cent buffalo wings on Fridays. Nina thought the spot was cute with its neon pink lights, red velvet sofas, and family-style seating that made it easier for everyone to get to know everybody. She expected the place to be packed with office workers, but there were lots of business executive types in suits with multi-thousand-dollar watches on their wrists. It was a place where anyone felt at home. Nina definitely did.

Nina and Melanie didn't sit at the family-style tables but sat at the bar where most of the action was. The loud bass sounds from the DJ booth flowed throughout the lounge, raising the energy through the roof.

"Are there places like this where you come from?" Melanie asked as they sipped on luscious mango-flavored margaritas.

"Yeah, but they close at like 10 P.M." Nina enjoyed the view from the bar. Several groups of people were trying to do the electric slide. Nina wasn't about to go there because she had on four-inch heels. She tossed her hair away from her eyes. "I'm just gonna slide to the bathroom for a second." She thought it would be a perfect time to try Dee or even call Ahmasi. She hadn't forgotten about what she needed to ask him.

"Ahmasi, it's Nina," she said as she found a quiet spot in the bathroom.

"Whatsup, baby girl."

"We need to talk."

"Everything cool?"

"I spoke to my soon-to-be ex-husband," Nina said, rolling her eyes. She leaned against the bathroom stall.

"So?"

"Do you know a Trent? That's his name."

"Trent, Trent, Trent—" Ahmasi tried to recall.

"He says he owes you some money?" Nina asked, her voice lowering as some women walked in.

"Oh, that's your husband? Old money bags," Ahmasi said, laughing. "Yeah, we had a little thing going."

"What thing?"

"I mean, you know I had a little weed hustle. Back in the day, I lent him a couple of Gs."

"How did you know him?"

"He knew my pops and I was in Houston to see some peeps. My pops gave me his info and—"

"And he just asked you for a few Gs just like that?"

"I had a loan shark business. Yeah, he did."

"How much?" Nina flushed the toilet to drown out her words.

"Like ten thousand dollars. And funny thing is, I've been trying to get my hands on that nigga. I haven't been able to find his ass."

Nina's stomach trembled. She hated Trent, but she certainly didn't want anything bad to happen. "What do you mean, Ahmasi?"

"Look, Trent and I will work this out. Did he say when he'll have my dough?"

"He said something about getting it to you."

"Good. Sorry you in the middle of this."

"I mean, what are the odds for me to go thousands of miles away and meet my husband's nemesis."

"I will be his nemesis if I don't get my money."

Nina flushed the toilet again as the women left. "I don't want anything to do with it. That is Trent's business."

"That's what I'm saying. It shouldn't interfere with what's going on between us, right?"

Nina stopped for a moment. She was pissed at Trent. Somehow his messiness had followed her here to a town where she thought she could get away and start over. She didn't want him getting in the way of anything. She wanted to stop talking to Ahmasi on her own account if an issue came up, not because of Trent. If he and Trent were working it out, then that was fine, she thought. "We're okay for now. Just promise me you won't ask me about him."

"About who?"

"Good." Nina smiled as she prepped her hair in the mirror. She had on jeans and a white button-on spring eyelet blouse with a fashionable cinch at the waist. She liked her look. She was slowly becoming more New York by the day.

"Where are you?" Ahmasi asked, hearing music.

"At Wish."

"How is it?"

"It's okay."

"Can I swing by?" he asked with a sigh. "I kind of miss you."

Nina didn't know what to say, but she didn't want him to come by. "I'm leaving soon."

"Can you call me when you leave?"

"Ahmasi, I may be tired. I'll call you when I get home, though," she said, with a strange feeling that he was keeping tabs on her.

"When can we see each other?" he asked.

Nina thought to herself that they'd just seen each other a few days ago. She wondered how attached Ahmasi was getting. "Not sure," she said, combing her hair some.

"How about you come over tonight? I got some good movies we can watch," he said excitedly.

"When do we ever watch television together?" Nina smiled.

"I'll call you when I leave here." Nina clicked off the phone, a bit annoyed. She thought maybe it was her decision to date Lamont, but maybe she did need to slow things down with Ahmasi after all. Except, the sex was too damn good.

When she returned to the bar, Melanie was there talking up the handsome bartender, her wedding ring shining under the bright lights. Nina swore she saw them exchange numbers. Nina sat down beside Melanie who gave her a coy look. "How's your divorce going, by the way?"

"Please," Nina said, crossing her legs, "I don't even want to talk about that. Trent's dirty laundry is everywhere. I can't seem to escape it."

"Like what?" Melanie asked.

"He owes some guy I met here some money. That's so embarrassing, and it's downright annoying that he always seems to turn up wherever I am!"

"I know what you mean." Melanie gazed straight ahead at the array of liquor and wine bottles behind the bar. "Pablo and I don't even speak anymore unless he asks what's for dinner. Everywhere I go, he has to know who, what, when, where, and how."

Nina didn't exactly see the correlation, but she let Melanie have her say. "I don't know where I'd be if I had spent another day with him. There's nothing worse than being married and feeling alone."

"Tell me about it," Melanie said, stirring her drink.

"I left my mama to marry him, but he turned into my mama," Nina added.

They both laughed as they comforted themselves with more drinks.

Melanie shook her head. "Sometimes we are a lot like our parents."

"I'm not. I don't want my man living off me. Mr. Darrell works for my mama. He can do absolutely nothing for her. Nothing."

"You are so lucky that you can start over. I know if I left Pablo, he would kill me."

"Come on, Melanie. That's a little too much," Nina said as a few people squeezed into the seats next to them at the bar.

Melanie laughed uncomfortably. "Well, yeah, but they say love makes you do crazy things."

Then Nina asked, "Have you ever dated anyone at the job?"

Melanie couldn't swallow her drink fast enough. "Not at Serenity. Delores don't play that. I think if she had a man she would understand what it's like. Just because she's single doesn't mean that's what we want, too."

Nina dabbed a little lotion on her short red-painted fingers. The music was getting better, but Nina wasn't in the mood to dance. "I was just asking," Nina said, putting the tube away.

Melanie scooted her stool closer to Nina's. "So, who asked you?"

"Nobody," Nina said, wanting badly to get Melanie's advice.

"Come on, girl, tell me. Okay, okay, if you don't want to, we can talk about it like it's other people."

"So there's this client who keeps coming on to this girl. He is fine as all get out, but she's worried her boss will find out. What should she do?"

"Hmmm," Melanie said as she put down her drink. She scratched her head. "Maybe she should pass him on to another girl at the job?"

"No." Nina giggled, and tapped Melanie playfully on the shoulder. "Not sure she'll be interested."

"What is he like?"

"He is paid because he left her a hundred-dollar tip."

"What!" Melanie slammed her hand on the bar. "The most I ever got was fifteen dollars. Whoever that chick is, is crazy. She need to step up her game. Damn it, give me her number. I'll talk to her."

Nina smiled at the bartender who was throwing them looks because of their dramatic antics. "What about Delores?"

"Shit, Delores would take him for herself, if she could. Tell this girl to go on the date."

Nina nodded as they finished their drinks, then headed for the dance floor. She was thankful that the electric slide had expired, and they could dance to real songs. Besides the Teacup Lounge, she hadn't been anywhere else. She only wished that Wish had a magic genie bottle to make all her wishes come true.

ten

Ahmasi almost shit in his pants when Nina asked him about Trent. He had met Trent years ago before he was married. Trent used to buy drugs from him—crack cocaine and weed. It was only after he married that Ahmasi heard he had cleaned up. But Trent was his number one customer for a while when he was living in Houston. Ahmasi wasn't as new as Nina, but he had been in New York City for only a few years. His background didn't allow him to get a regular job, so he relied on poetry and messenger jobs. But he didn't forget that Trent owed him big-time for thousands and he was determined to get it. He thought that maybe God was cutting him a break by turning Nina up in his life. If it wasn't for that, he probably wouldn't have been able to track Trent down ever.

But there was something more about Nina. It was a relationship that was sexual, but more dangerous than any real relationship he'd had. He would be Nina's man, if she asked him to. In fact, he wanted to be. He wanted to know where she was when she wasn't with him. He wanted to know what she was wearing when they were apart, what she was eating, and what she was thinking.

Ahmasi brought the Nina-scented flat sheets to his nose and inhaled. *Poison.* Ahmasi smiled, raised himself out of the bed, and placed his feet on the floor. It was 11 P.M. On the nightstand was Nina's purse with her cell phone sticking out of it. It had beeped a few minutes ago, but she didn't answer it. He wrestled with the idea that he should take a look just in case it rang again.

"You need to get some food in here," Nina said as she walked in from the kitchen with a bowl of dry cornflakes. She sat on the bed as she and Ahmasi dipped their fingers into it interchangeably.

"I thought you had filled yourself up on buffalo wings at that spot."

"Yeah, but when I drink, I get even hungrier."

"But you're not drunk now."

"I know," Nina snickered. "I guess I'm just being greedy."

Their tongues found their way into each other's mouths. Ahmasi unbuttoned the blue shirt of his that Nina was wearing. She hadn't planned to come by tonight, but found herself not wanting to be alone either.

Her breasts dangled in front of him like ripened peaches. He spread his tongue over her big nipples, sucking her entire breast into his mouth. He couldn't resist Nina, nor could she resist him. He wanted to eat every morsel of her. As he lay on his back, Nina held his throbbing dick in her hand. He hadn't asked her to suck him because he knew how much work that would entail. But tonight, she seemed up for it. She crawled down between his thighs and brought the head of his dick into her mouth, moving it in and out. He bent one knee and spread his legs out as she acquainted herself with the heavy task at hand. Nina glued her lips over his entire length, leaving only an inch or two at the base. Her face was buried between his Ivory soap–scented thighs. Eventually, she managed to get the remaining inches into her mouth. Her chin bumped against his balls as she pumped him of his energy. She slipped him out of her mouth and patted her tongue around the head, lapping up his sweet juices. Ahmasi was a vegan, and fruits were a large part of his diet.

He grabbed her head with both of his hands, trying to control her motions.

Ahmasi twisted Nina's hair around her head as he said, "That's right, show the dick some love." He pulled her hair back off her face. "I wanna see all my dick in your mouth," he whispered. He was weak and about to bust. He was in no way in charge here. Nina was. She was feeding off of him everything she needed, and everything he wanted. She promised herself this was the last time.

Before he came, Ahmasi turned her over and busily sucked her pussy until the sheets were soaked. Now that she was nice and open, Ahmasi pushed his way inside her with fanatical thrusts that landed them both on the floor. But that didn't stop anything. Nina hopped on Ahmasi's dick and rode him with her feet firmly planted on the floor. He held on to the foot of his bed and let her enjoy his stick for her pleasure.

"Oh, God, I can't take this," Nina moaned as her face was covered with sweat-drenched clumps of hair. "I can't, I can't," she kept saying as her gyrating motions got wilder and wilder. His dick was so hard it hurt. She squeezed her pussy muscles around him, making his eyes pop out. Ahmasi wanted to connect with her, but her eyes were closed as she collapsed on top of him.

Nina made it back to her apartment in Brooklyn by 2 A.M. As soon as she walked in, she saw Ms. Bauer in the hallway.

"Good mornin', Ms. Bauer," Nina said as the older woman slipped on her glasses with a dissatisfied look.

"Young lady, what time is it?"

Nina turned around in case there was someone else. For a moment, she felt like she was being checked by the house madam.

"Sorry if I woke you up, Ms. Bauer." Nina turned the lock on her door. She wanted to sleep. She wasn't in the frame of mind to hold any coherent conversations. She could barely walk.

Then Ms. Bauer's tone changed. "Are you hungry?" she asked from the top of the steps, her hair topped with pink sponge rollers.

Nina played with the keys in her hand. She was famished, and this could be a good time to ask Ms. Bauer why she was telling folks her business. *Or was it?* she thought. Nina looked up and said, "If you don't mind?"

"Come on up here," Ms. Bauer said with a friendly smile. That was a first, thought Nina. As she climbed the steps, she thought about Ahmasi and how good he gave it to her tonight. She felt like she could stick a basketball up there right now. As she took her time walking up the steps, little air bubbles came out of her, and she prayed that Ms. Bauer couldn't hear them.

Nina sat down in the kitchen, which was beautifully adorned with blue and white wallpaper. The blue and white checkered tablecloth looked like something one would find in a country home catalog. Ms. Bauer sauntered around in her big, fluffy, green slippers. Nina noticed how the slippers matched perfectly with her green terry cloth robe. The smell of corn bread and the scent of spices was everywhere. Nina figured it was being up this late that made it possible for Ms. Bauer to snoop around.

"Now, I don't know what ya like to eat, but I got some corn bread, some slices of chicken, and a bit of sweet potato mash with brown sugar," Ms. Bauer said as she looked in the refrigerator.

Nina thought about how sweet and old she looked. She felt bad about wanting to drill her.

"Oh, that's plenty, thank you." Nina's eyes got big at the beautiful presentation of the food Ms. Bauer put on the plate. She even garnished the sweet potato mash with freshly grated cinnamon.

"Here you go, baby," Ms. Bauer said as she laid down the hot plate. Her round, wrinkled light brown face beamed as Nina attacked the food.

"Child, when was the last time you ate?" Ms. Bauer asked, rubbing her fatty, brown-spotted hands together.

"Yesterday afternoon, but I had a long night," Nina said, spooning up the sweet delicious mash.

"Hmph, a long night?" Ms. Bauer looked troubled. "What kind of night?"

Nina glanced at Ms. Bauer. *How was she gonna ask another grown woman about her night? It is my business!* "Why do you ask, Ms. Bauer?" Nina was trying to be cordial, but it was time to set Ms. Bauer straight.

"Oh, child," Ms. Bauer laughed. "Don't get all stuffy on me. I'm just trying to get to know you. When you moved in here, you was ten pounds heavier, at least. It don't look like you taking care of yourself."

"I'm fine, Ms. Bauer," Nina said, wishing she could take the food downstairs. She ate faster.

"I'm gonna give you some food to take with you."

Nina let her prepare a few plates and, in a separate container, she threw in a slice of yellow cake that she had baked earlier. Perhaps Ms. Bauer took interest in her because she had no children of her own, Nina thought. She tried not to take her prying too personally, but she had to know.

"Why haven't you invited me to eat before? I've been living in your house for a few months now," Nina said.

"I wasn't too sure if you wanted that. But I thought about it and I know Dee. Dee is a good woman. I told her I would look out for you. So I said, no time better than the present."

"I see," Nina said as she stood up from the table. "Did you also tell her about my friend Ahmasi?"

Ms. Bauer snapped the cover in the Tupperware with the chicken. "Oh, Nina, I didn't mean to pry. When I saw you leave that night with that guy on the bike, I began to think some things. I don't know if he's a good one. So I told Dee."

"What do you mean?"

"I don't want to say no more but that we older folk have a certain innate sense about these things. Just be careful," Ms. Bauer said, patting Nina on the shoulder as she handed her several containers of food.

"Thank you for the food, Ms. Bauer." Nina didn't want to be rude. She knew she needed to take it up with Dee and not harass the poor old woman. Nina left and walked back down to her apartment. As she settled in she thought about what Ms. Bauer could mean. But she agreed that she had to be careful.

eleven

Tonight was Nina's date with Lamont, two weeks later at Gramercy Tavern. She knew instantly that she felt a different kind of attraction to him. He seemed like the type of man who she could take seriously, and he would take her seriously, too. His timing wasn't bad either, she thought. She'd decided that as good as he made her feel, she had to wean herself from Ahmasi, if she could. But she still had to find out if Lamont was all he appeared to be.

"How long have you been into massage therapy? You like it?" Lamont asked over dinner in the main room of the restaurant.

"I love it and I want to have my own business one day. The trick is that you have to be impersonal about it, almost clinical. Very little eye contact helps."

"You mean you have to be good at hiding your feelings?" he asked.

Nina hesitated. "Yeah, I do," she said simply and left it at that. She was a pro at bottling up her feelings and letting things go, but every day she found herself speaking out more.

Lamont smiled at Nina when the waiter brought the menus. She wore a sleeveless, red chiffon dress that went past her knees. She'd picked it up at a consignment shop in Park Slope and it fit her svelte body perfectly. She had a conservative look, very different from what she'd wear hanging with Ahmasi. This was how she wanted to always look: polished, stylish, and classy.

The waiter introduced them to the specials of the evening. Lamont gave him their orders happily. Nina wasn't as interested in eating as she was in getting to know all about Lamont.

Nina let out a laugh as she thought about an incident at the spa. "One teenage boy asked me if I could massage all the players on his football team. He was convinced that my massages earned him the most touchdowns in school history. He had a bad shoulder. His whole team ended up sending me letters and flowers begging me to treat them, but I couldn't," Nina said as she chose a fork to cut into her spinach.

"Here you go," Lamont said, handing her the appropriate salad fork. He let it go gradually as she took it from him, a bit embarrassed.

"I never knew there were so many forks to choose from." Nina giggled, feeling a little goofy. But he seemed to like it.

"You're a beautiful woman; I can see how you can draw lots of attention," he said, setting his dreamy eyes on Nina.

"Thank you," Nina said. "I certainly got your attention, but it wasn't what I expected."

Lamont blushed. "That's because I was thinking about you as you massaged me." He laughed. "Nothing too perverted, but let's just say I was on fantasy island."

Nina chewed her food and listened as the compliments kept coming. Everything he was saying, thought Nina, was an answer to some question she had.

"I was thinking about how to get closer to you," Lamont said. "When a man has that feeling, nothing rests until he can explore the possibility."

"What feeling?"

"The feeling that you've met a special woman and that our paths crossed for a reason. I could've met ten women after our first appointment, but they would've meant nothing because all I would be thinking about was you."

Nina patted her chest lightly. She thought she was about to choke. She had to restrain herself from jumping across the table and tackling him with hugs and kisses. She loved his intensity. It was sexy and bold.

"Did you meet ten women?" she asked.

"Maybe four, but all work-related." He laughed, his eyes glimmering with enjoyment. He eyed her as they went back to eating their salads.

Nina checked him out, too. His diamond-crusted Rolex watch had so much shine on it she thought she needed a visor. He wore sharp, wide-legged linen pants and an African-style tunic that looked like it had been made just for him. Nina stopped eating when the sommelier presented them with their wine selection. Lamont handed the cork to Nina to check for dryness. But she didn't know what it was for, and just put it down. The sommelier filled their glasses as they both watched.

Nina held up her glass and Lamont did, too. "To meeting, to life," Lamont said. "Cheers."

"Cheers," she said as their glasses clinked.

Lamont sipped the Spanish wine and asked, "So tell me, what do I have to do to see you on the regular?"

Nina thought that it was going to be easier said than done. "You may have to find a new massage therapist."

"Do I?" he asked.

"Let's be real here. There's no guarantee that this is gonna work out. You can't see me for a third time. We're not there yet for me to be giving free massages at your home—"

"I'll pay you," he retorted.

Nina grinned, as tempting as it was. "Let's just take it slow. For now, let's just have dinner."

"Okay, fine," Lamont said as he reached for his glass.

The waiter came and placed their steaming hot entrees in front of them.

Nina thought it was time to start quizzing him. She needed to know what she was putting her job on the line for. "Do you live with anyone?"

"No, I'm not into playing that house thing. The only woman living with me is gonna be my wife."

Nina nodded as she cut into her fettuccine. She liked that answer.

Before she could ask something else, he said, "So where do you hang out since you moved here?"

She realized he wasn't asking her about her divorce yet, which was good. She needed some time away from any talk of that.

"I go to this poetry thing at the Teacup Lounge. It's a nice, real laid-back kind of place."

Lamont twirled the pasta into his spoon. "The Teacup Lounge is still open? You like that place? It's a little grimy."

Nina smiled. "I know, but it's interesting."

Lamont signaled to the waiter for more water. "You're not meeting any *real* men at places like that. Men with money. You can't live off poetry."

"Well, I wasn't going to meet anybody," she said, immediately thinking of Ahmasi, but Lamont didn't have to know that.

"What do you do?" Nina asked, proud of herself for not seeming too eager to ask, though she was.

"I'm a corporate attorney for a law firm. Soon to be partner, I hope. It's a lot of hours, but the pay is ridiculous. Eventually, I'll branch out and do my own thing. I love to travel too much, and my schedule doesn't allow it as I'd like."

Nina had thought that he'd have a fancy job like that. She could just imagine the both of them jet-setting to luxurious resorts. She hadn't ever left the country. Her first time leaving the state of Texas was when she moved to New York. Traveling and being financially independent was how she always wanted to live. Nina put a piece of the pasta in her mouth. The way Lamont's eyes followed her mouth, she knew he would have done anything to be the sauce on her fork.

Then he flipped the topic on her.

"Do you have children?"

"No, do you?"

"No," Lamont said. "But I will."

"I'm not that big on kids, at least not right now."

"I'm not arguing with you on that one," he said, reaching for his wine and taking a long, slow sip. "What about your husband?"

"We're almost divorced. You mean ex," she corrected him. *Here we go,* she thought.

"Where's that at right now?"

"Well, he sent the papers to my lawyer, last I heard. But I haven't been able to reach my lawyer yet to find out what's next. But as far as I'm concerned, it's done," Nina said, dabbing the corner of her mouth. She wanted to keep the evening light. They had plenty of time to discuss Trent later.

"How long were you married?"

"Five years, but, Lamont, if you don't mind, I'd rather not ruin my appetite talking about that," Nina said, swirling her fork around her plate.

"Certainly," he said as he went back to eating. "But can I say one thing?"

Nina couldn't help but smirk at him. He was cute, so she found it difficult to get too easily annoyed with his assertiveness. "Go ahead."

"I was married, too."

For some reason, Nina felt some weight lift off her. But she wasn't as surprised as she thought she'd be because Lamont was attractive and successful. She thought that at least once someone had dragged him down the aisle. But she didn't probe because it seemed like he knew what he wanted to say.

"We were married for a minute. We rushed it. Thank God, no kids were involved," Lamont said.

She respected him for being so open with her.

"And I'm not scared to do it again. I just want to get it right, or as best as I can."

"Same here," Nina said, feeling a firm connection with him. "I probably should've never married." She stuffed a forkful of pasta in her mouth.

"You just didn't have the right man who could love you like you deserve."

Nina thought that she had no idea of what kind of love she needed, but she knew what she wanted it to feel like. After some time, they went back to their food and talked about less heavy-laden things, like the best place to get a pizza or best train car to sit in during peak hours, and how it was particularly key not to give anyone eye contact. She had learned that like every other place, New York City had its rules and science for survival, and she sure didn't want to break any.

After Lamont paid for dinner, he put his arm around her shoulders, and they strolled down Park Avenue. It was one of those perfect New York City late March nights where the air was light with moisture, but warm with spring. Lamont hailed a cab to take them to his home in Brooklyn. During the ride, Nina laid her head on his shoulder and dozed off. For a moment, she felt secure and taken care of. He knew when to push, and when to stop. He was open to her, and she could get used to that.

When they arrived in his Fort Greene multilevel brownstone on South Oxford Street, they worked on a second bottle of wine, nearly finishing it. Nina didn't want the evening to end. She enjoyed being with a man like Lamont who was successful and assertive about what he wanted. She also admired his style and grace. He had a third bottle of wine standing ready nearby. She was sure she surprised him at how well her slender frame held alcohol. She had been trained when she was young. She used to drink at her mother's weekly poker parties. She started at eleven, and they would bet how much more she could drink than the last time. That was the most fun she'd had with her family, until she realized how sick it made her. She and Lamont were just enjoying themselves, of course, and hoping some truth serum would help bring out anything they needed to know about each other. Nina thought, *Here he is, fine as the Lord is good, with a fabulous home, expensive furnishings, and single. Something has to be up.* She hoped that it wasn't what she was thinking. Single fine men were rumored to have short dicks or be gay. She was betting on the small dick.

They sat back on the couch and swayed to Miles Davis's "So What." The French doors to Lamont's deck were closed but the view of the full moon was entrancing. She scooted closer to him, letting her eyes gaze on his thick, smooth lips.

Lamont dimmed the lights, took Nina by the hand, and did some slow moves to the jazz that played. He touched her neck with his big, juicy lips. He did this slowly, giving her enough response time to stop him. She didn't, but she had to at some point. She wasn't ready for more yet. He brought his fingers to the slit opening of her dress. He undid a few buttons and kissed her shoulders. Their lips caught each other in the dark as their feet danced. She wrapped her arms around his neck and imagined that she was skating on ice. She ran her fingers down his face and into his mouth, and let him suck on them. In and out, she put one in and took one out. He reminded her of a hungry dog, sucking whatever finger was next. Lamont took a few steps back, their lips locked as they moved to the beat. He was leading the way to his master bedroom. They stepped along with the beat of the music as they walked down the hall.

"You ready for this?" he asked, holding her by her slender shoulders. In her mind, they had already had sex twice with all the rubbing she had done on his body during his appointments.

"No, I'm not," she said, taking his hands down. "Maybe I should go."

"Wait." Lamont walked up to her. "Can you stay?"

"Lamont, I'm just not ready to have sex. I really like you and—"

"We can just lie together. I would really like the company," he said, kissing behind her ears.

She could use the company, too, she thought. Nina sauntered back into the bedroom and Lamont gave her some clothes she could sleep in.

Lamont peeled off his shirt, pulled down his pants, neatly rolled both, and laid them on his armoire. He threw her a silly look. "I hate ironing."

Lamont showed Nina where the shower was. He had two bathrooms. They washed up for the evening and got themselves together before joining each other in bed.

Nina was nervous. She trusted Lamont, but she didn't trust herself. All he had to do was breathe on her too hard, and she'd be fired up. But she had to talk herself down. He looked like a good man, and she didn't want to ruin it by having sex so soon. She was still having sex with Ahmasi, and hadn't cut that off yet, officially. But she knew Lamont was the one she wanted. Lamont climbed into bed beside her and kissed Nina's mouth gently. The light from the nightstand shone on her body that was dressed in a long T-shirt, boxers, and socks. He pressed up against her and inhaled the clean scent of her freshly washed hair. She felt his hardness on her back. "Good night," he said into her ear.

"Good night," Nina responded as she nestled in his arms.

twelve

A few days later on Monday, Nina was staring at the signed documents mailed by Dee's Houston lawyer. It was official. She was no longer Nina Raines, but back to Nina Bettus. The "Bettus" part of her name was something she hadn't used for years, so it felt foreign. She felt displaced, but what made her feel better was that she had her daddy's name back. Now, she had it in her power to make him proud and stop that cycle of abuse and betrayal in her family. She was on her own again, in more ways than just location. She was a free woman, but there were still some ties that bind.

Nina tried Dee for the hundredth time, and she finally got a hold of her. "Were you ever gonna call?" she asked when she heard Dee's voice. She wanted to be angry, but she was too happy to make any room for that.

"Nina! Child, I have been to Detroit and two other cities for small business conferences and lingerie shows. I have been so busy doing my thing. I am so sorry we couldn't talk. Every time I tried to call you, it'd go straight to voice mail until I finally gave up."

Dee hated leaving voice messages. "Same thing would happen to me when I tried to call you!"

"Girl, did you get the papers?"

"I sure did. Amen and thank you, Jesus." Nina laughed, kicking her foot in the air.

"I'm about to catch the Holy Ghost on that one." Dee joined Nina in their laugh. But then Nina remembered.

"You know, the funniest thing happened," Nina said, putting the papers down.

"What?"

"Did you tell Trent that I am seeing someone named Ahmasi?"

"Girl, we need to talk about that," Dee began as her voice grew louder on the phone. "He cornered me one day in my shop talking about how he needed to get your information. I told him he'd have to go over my dead body. He got me so mad, I did kind of blurt out you was seeing someone named Ahmasi. I know it was dumb of me to say the name."

"Why'd you say the name?" Nina asked, confused as ever.

"I don't know. I thought it would make him even angrier because it sounded so exotic and different. Plus, he pissed me off, coming in my shop and disrespecting me and my customers."

Nina quieted for a moment as she took a deep breath. "Well, I can't officially apologize for Trent anymore because we are not married, but maybe things happen for a reason."

"Did he do something?"

"He told me that he owes Ahmasi money. I asked Ahmasi about it, and lo and behold, he knows Trent and he confirmed it. They had some little business thing he didn't get into. He seemed pretty upset that Trent owed him so much, but tried to play it cool for me."

"Oh, my God, so what kind of guy is Ahmasi? I mean, you know we can't rely on Trent to pay back anybody, ever."

"Trent told me that he will pay him."

"How much is it?"

"It's ten thousand dollars, Dee. And I know for a fact Trent has the money."

"I heard he's driving around town with a Benz. What if Trent doesn't pay this guy back? Money makes people do bad things."

Nina blew down on the phone. "I don't know how Trent got me caught up in this." Dee's concern made Nina even more concerned.

"Nina, you may need to disconnect yourself from this Ahmasi guy because you don't know the full story. You don't want to get in the middle of no money business."

"I know."

"I'm serious, girl! You need to deal with that right after we hang up. Out of all the men in New York you find yourself with another loser."

"Oh, Dee, don't go there," Nina said, offended by her remark. "How was I supposed to know? We are just *friends.*"

"You fucked him."

Nina paused. "Yeah, I did."

"And I bet it's *good.* Brother got you under dick-motized or something."

Dee knew the cards like they were her own. "We had sex before all this came out. He makes my body feel alive again. I was just having fun."

"Okay, well, obviously the fun is over. Find another man. Girl, you gonna have me worried about you now."

"I know what I have to do about Ahmasi. Not just because of

Trent, but because I met another man who is really nice, a gentleman, and he has a job and is financially secure."

"Okay, then. Go handle that. Please, just get rid of this Ahmasi cat before anything else. I don't trust Trent."

They caught up on a few other things before they hung up. Nina knew that Ahmasi wouldn't take it lightly.

"How's your friend doing with that client you were telling me about?" Melanie asked later in the day at work.

"Let's just give it up. It's me and I'm busted," Nina said as they both stole some time in between clients.

"So, how is he?"

"Good. I can't tell you his name though. We talk almost every day and he says he has a surprise for me this weekend," Nina whispered.

"He knows about your divorce?"

"Yeah, he was divorced, too."

"That's what they all say," Melanie said, as cynical as ever. "What about the poet guy? I liked him."

"It's just sex, but it's getting a little complicated."

"Girl, as long as he's not Hispanic, you have nothing to worry about. I'm telling you I got one right now who is really tripping. I didn't tell you this, but Javier is my husband's friend. He's always threatening to tell Pablo about us. If he can't have me, no one can."

Nina turned around. "Have you seen the news? Hispanic men rule the crimes of passion segment," she said with a laugh.

Melanie joined her. "Anyhow, how many people do you have left today?"

"I have Mr. Sandsman. He is the cutest littlest old man I've ever seen," Nina said. "He'll be here any minute."

"You always get the good customers." Melanie grinned as they dispersed when they heard Delores next door.

They both walked out to the reception area and picked up their clients. Mr. Sandsman was an eighty-two-year-old retired pilot. Another male massage therapist at the spa had him and warned that he falls asleep on the table and his breathing needed to be checked every few minutes.

"Hi, Mr. Sandsman, follow me," Nina said with a glowing smile. She wore gloves with Mr. Sandsman because intense psoriasis made his flaky, white skin chip off like paint. No one liked him because of that, but Nina felt she had to do the best job possible. She wanted to make sure the gloves she wore were the smoothest she could find because she didn't want to compromise his experience.

"Hey, Nina!" Mr. Sandsman said when she approached him. He had on a weathered, navy blue suit that stopped at his ankles. He may have looked weathered too, but everyone was aware that Mr. Sandsman was wealthy and owned a million-dollar town home on the Upper East Side. "I waited all week to get booked with you. I'm going mountain climbing this week and want to be loose in the caboose!"

"Great." Nina laughed along with him.

"I heard you were the best," Mr. Sandsman said as he walked alongside her.

She could tell he was going to be a talkative client and breathing wasn't something she'd have to worry about.

"These turkey sandwiches from the deli are so good," Nina said as Melanie and she sat on one of the benches outside their office on Bleeker Street. Melanie was eating food she brought from home. To Nina, aside from the rice, everything else was unrecognizable.

"I made some platanos last night and Pablo ate them all. The bastard couldn't even leave me one," she said with a grimace.

"What is with you two?"

"He's too jealous and he drinks like a damn fish," Melanie complained.

"So aren't you scared that Javier is gonna tell Pablo one day? They are friends."

"First of all, Javier is in this country illegally. I told him if he ever tried to tell Pablo that I would personally see to it that his ass be shipped back in one of those cargo boats. He would rather die than go back to DR."

"That is what I'm saying! What if he tries to hurt you?"

"Girl, I got my Santeria candles and with one, two, three, he will forget all about me. But I don't want him to," she said, grinning. "So have you gone down on the poet yet?"

"Is that all you care about?" Nina joked.

"I'm just still amazed—and envious."

"I did. I took it inch by inch, very slowly. It was crazy and we were out of control just feeding off each other," Nina said, watching the passersby on the street. "But he's getting too attached."

"You'll be surprised at how many things you can control," Melanie said with a wink. "You can have the other guy you went to dinner with in a heartbeat and get rid of this Ahmasi in a nice way." Nina knew what Melanie was suggesting, but she wondered why Melanie didn't use it to help herself.

thirteen

Nina milled around her apartment trying to find her comb. It was a cozy, well-kept apartment, with hardwood floors, a brick exposure over the stove, and large, wide windows. She didn't have much furniture or a bed yet. A mattress and box spring were what she slept on. She didn't even own a TV set because something told her that this was all temporary and she wasn't sure if she liked living under Ms. Bauer. Despite it all, she made sure her bathroom was hooked up with pretty candles, a red throw carpet, and fancy bottles she had bought at the ninety-nine-cent store to hold all her special needs.

"Hey, honey," Ms. Bauer called from the top of the steps when Nina was walking out the door. She didn't know how this woman timed her exits perfectly.

"Hi, Ms. Bauer. How are you?" Nina said, stopping to greet her.

"I'm fine, thank you. Just up here straightening out some things. If you get in late again, feel free to knock. I got a nice meat loaf

I'm making you'll absolutely adore," she said, holding her hands to her chest.

"Okay. If I get back in time, Ms. Bauer, I'll stop by. See you later," Nina said as she made her way out the door and down the steps. As she walked down the block, she turned around and saw Ms. Bauer looking out the window with a disapproving look. Maybe, Nina thought, it was her short jeans skirt.

At the Teacup Lounge, it was just Nina and Ahmasi at his table tonight. Nina didn't miss Isis or Sura at all. She had some serious issues she wanted to talk to Ahmasi about. She wanted a clean slate, but he seemed so happy and relaxed, she didn't know when would be a good time.

A loud R & B tune vibrated off the walls. Nina could barely hear herself think, let alone hear Ahmasi talk. Nina thought he was looking extra cute tonight with dark blue jeans and a Sean John sweater, and his locks tied into a high ponytail.

"You know I didn't want to change my sheets this weekend because they still smell like you. I need you," Ahmasi revealed suddenly.

Nina grabbed a handful of pretzels from a bowl. A couple squeezed in next to them, drawing Ahmasi and Nina closer under the darkness of the lounge. "Did you get your money yet?"

Ahmasi took his arm from around her and tensed up. "I'm supposed to be going down to Houston to get it."

"Why?"

"He ain't sending it yet for some reason. If the money don't come to me, I have to go to the money."

Nina caught the blank look in his eyes. He didn't seem pleased at all about it.

"When do you leave?" she asked.

"Not sure, but I don't want to talk about that right now. Didn't you say you didn't want to hear about it?"

"I guess," she answered. "But it's really bothering me—"

Ahmasi licked his lips. "I love it when you get upset. You get these little wrinkles around the corners of your mouth. Cute." He leaned over and planted a warm, soft kiss on her lips.

Nina's mouth flew open. "I don't think I can see you anymore, Ahmasi—"

"What you mean?" He smiled, moving his hands farther up her thighs. He whispered in her ear. "Can I suck on that pussy one more time?"

Nina tilted her head slightly to the side as the warm air of his breath tickled her earlobes. She felt tingles down her leg. She wouldn't mind one more romp.

"It ain't that serious, baby. Just one more time. Then you can go your way and I'll go mine," he said, his fingers traveling farther up her thigh to her panties.

Nina hadn't been finger-popped since high school. His thumb stuck its way in and out and all around under the table. She parted her legs some more as he explored her soft wetness with his touch. He had her in a clutch and she did want some more for the road.

Then Nina heard his name over the mike. It startled her, and she almost kicked the table down. "Ahmasi, they're calling your name onstage," she said to him. His eyes were fixated on her like he couldn't get enough. Nina moved his hand from between her legs when his name was called again.

"Oh, shit." Ahmasi jumped his thin, lightweight body out of the darkened booth. He walked to the stage with a cool swagger and stopped to say some "hellos" to a few of his peeps at the crowded tables in the front.

Sammy, the announcer, repeated for the third time, "And now, our headliner, Ahmasi . . ."

Before he jumped onstage, Ahmasi whispered something to the light-skinned waitress with the red 'fro, and within minutes Nina had a platter of her favorite at the table—seasoned French fries.

"Everybody feeling all right?" They roared back, cheering.

He set his sight on Nina, and recited his first of several poems.

"Break that body over me
Like the dam over thee
I want to pour my essence
Into being
One with you
Stars blink, I sink
In deeper with you
Not wanting you
Loving you
Break that body over me
That my cells become three
Pouring my essence into you
Loving me
When I hate you
Wanting you and the pain
The blame, the heat,
The beat that you can't keep
Breaking into you cumming into me
When you hate me
Sinking in our pain
One with you."

Nina felt like crap. But she wasn't going to let Ahmasi's words give her any second thoughts. She planned to go back to his place, but that was all. After tonight, he was moving on, and so was she.

At the end of the night, Nina was at Ahmasi's place for the last time. He kissed her along her Poison-scented collarbone as he turned the doorknob. He then gently bit into her neck and ran his hands up her blouse.

She took it off for him, exposing round, full breasts that stood out for him to do as he pleased. They tumbled to the ground still holding each other. Nina grabbed his head, squeezing it as he licked her nipples. He bit them. Gently, then hard.

"Ooh," Nina moaned in pain and delight. He made her feel as nasty as she wanted to be.

He sniffed and licked her underarm. It made her giggle. He bit the sides of her breasts as she yanked his pants down.

"Ahmasi," she called out to him. She wanted a good quickie, but he was taking his time. He slid down her black panties and smelled their white cotton center. He rubbed his face into her pussy and tasted some of her wetness. She called out his name again, but he seemed consumed by her. She wanted to get into bed. But he ate her like he wanted to become a part of her, like her next breath. He pressed his head deeper into her dark space. She clenched her knees against his ears. Nina's legs felt like two strings of spaghetti limp with anticipation and seventh heaven.

Nina gripped his shoulders to pull him up when he was done. She wanted him to stick her up like she stole something.

He slid his fingers inside her, tasting them like she was coated with honey. Her knees lost their grip around him. She begged him, "Please, put it in." She needed to be filled up with his weight. He turned her over, and tossed her salad and her mind, leaving her ass glistening. She rose on her knees and turned around to look at him. He looked like an African prince about to mount a horse, with his deep-set eyes and tea-black skin. He spread her slim thighs and slid his dick inside her doggy style, making her pussy quiver with every stroke. It hurt more than usual; it was like he had grown another inch and that made her nervous. Sensing her tightness, he leaned over and gently caressed her pussy until she had a nice, wide spread. He pumped her good, and she pumped back good.

Nina's knees finally gave out as Ahmasi lay flat on top of her, biting her shoulders and her ears, until they both climaxed at the same time, something Nina had never experienced before. They fell asleep on the bed together, with him wrapped around her like a comma.

When Nina woke up the following morning, she crept around quietly for her clothes. She dressed and looked around for anything she might be forgetting. As she combed her hair in the bathroom and applied some gloss, she saw Ahmasi's reflection in the mirror.

His dreads tousled all over his head, he asked, "Are you sure this is the last time?"

Nina inhaled deeply. "Yes, it is."

"It wasn't good last night?"

"It was excellent, like it always is. I just need some time to myself. My divorce is final and I need to get my life back in order," she said, turning around.

He held her. "If you ever change your mind—"

"It's okay, Ahmasi. Let's just leave it like this," she said in a firm tone that said she wasn't backing down. She wasn't going to live her life on anyone's terms but her own. Nina grabbed her bag and walked to the door.

"I'm leaving for Houston in a few days—"

"Have a safe trip. Take care." Nina planted a kiss on his cheek. "And if it's any consolation, you were the best I ever had," she said, and walked out with an extra swing in her step.

fourteen

The following day, on a Saturday, as Nina soaked in her tub with lavender-scented bubbles, she thought about Lamont. She had only been out with him once, and missed him. He was patient with her. But she felt she was ready to take that next step with him. She wanted more than anything to have a normal relationship with a man. She wanted to go shopping with him, bathe with him, watch television with him, and even argue with him. She wanted everything that a relationship entailed without the heartache. But she understood that with the sweet came the sour and Lamont may have been the only one she'd want to be with when the sour came.

Lamont told her he was cooking his specialty tonight—sherried chicken breasts and yellow rice. He said the dish was "elegant," just like her. If only, she thought. She had never had a man cook for her unless she could count the eggs and ham Trent would cook every blue moon. Besides that, they'd be at her mother's house for food most of the time.

After her bath, she quickly dressed to meet Lamont at Eve's Garden, a gourmet specialty store on Montague Street in Brooklyn. He thought it was a good idea that they pick out what he needed for their meal together. She checked herself for the final time in the mirror. She wore a comfortable, black sleeveless dress, bought at Target, that draped her curves front and back. It looked expensive with black heeled sandals that could easily transition into an evening outfit.

At around 6:30 P.M., she and Lamont met inside the market. They perused the aisles of fresh greens, gourmet chutneys, and artisan cheeses. Nina and Lamont must have been in the store for only fifteen minutes when they met a familiar face.

"Hello, Nina," Delores said as she pushed a cart with a small child in it. Nina wasn't even aware that she had children.

Lamont stood beside Nina as Nina smiled and said, "Good to see you, Delores," through her clenched teeth. It wasn't good to see her, Nina thought. "Is this adorable baby yours?"

Delores smiled quickly at Lamont. "No, this is my niece, Ada." Delores couldn't take her eyes off Nina. "What are you doing around here?"

"Oh, just shopping with a friend," Nina said, trying her best to avoid introducing Lamont.

But Delores caught on. She adjusted her pink and white striped blouse. "Good to see you, Mr. Franklin. Do you live in the area?"

Lamont shook her hand. "A little farther up in Fort Greene on South Oxford."

"I live just two blocks north of there," Delores said with a phony grin. "Well, I'll let you two do what people do on rainy Saturday afternoons. Enjoy. See you Monday, Nina."

This couldn't be any worse, Nina thought. Delores was the last person she thought she'd see.

"You okay?" Lamont asked as they walked down the spices aisle.

"I just want to get out of here, fast. Delores didn't look like she was buying the friend bit at all."

"Can she really fire you because of that? We can get a lawyer."

"She can. It's her company policy. I don't want to get the law involved in this because it's her company. She makes the rules that makes for good business. I'll just have to explain on Monday."

She and Lamont finished up their shopping and paid at the register. Lamont put his arm around her as they left the store. She didn't want him to move it. He made everything seem all right, for today, at least.

When they got to his place, Nina followed him into the kitchen. He had on neatly pressed khakis and a black buttoned shirt.

"I got a little head start on things earlier, but didn't do much," he said, setting a succulent kiss on her mouth. "Maybe you can help me cook?"

"No, Lamont. I cannot cook worth my life. But I can help," Nina said, laying down a brown grocery bag on the kitchen counter.

"You never cooked for your ex-husband?" He whipped out a white apron from a drawer and wrapped it around himself. Nina helped him tie it in the back. She thought he sounded like he could be high maintenance, but she was up for it.

"I would cook some turkey wings from time to time, but that's all I know."

"No one ever taught you how to cook anything else?" He laughed. "What about your mom?"

She didn't want to utter a word about her mother. As far as she was concerned, she was written off. "Everything I know I basically taught myself." She sighed and said, "Look, I'll be happy to watch you cook. Pass you a tomato or something. But I really don't want to mess this up. Trust me."

He looked at her like she was making it all up to be cute. He pressed her up against the counter and kissed her lips again. Her eyes rolled back for a minute, because even his breath tasted and smelled good.

"Can I teach you?" he asked.

She had almost forgotten how persistent he could be. She looked around the kitchen again. It didn't seem like he was going to start without her. "What the hell," she said.

He rubbed his hands together and wrapped an extra apron around her waist. "Do you know how to use a knife?" he asked as he rinsed off the cutting board.

"Of course I do," she said, her chest sticking out with surety.

He handed her a knife and an onion. "You can do that, then."

Nina stared at the large knife and it dawned on her what he meant by using a knife. She stabbed the onion in the middle.

Lamont laughed and took the knife from her. "Damn, I would love to see how you treat your enemies. I meant cutting skills. Like this," he said and showed her. He set the onion on the cutting board and sliced it in half. "Give me your hand."

Nina put her hand on the knife and he put his hand over hers as he led her to cut and dice the onion up into bitty pieces. His hands moved hers so quickly she closed her eyes a few times. But when she opened them, the onions were cut up and no one had gotten hurt.

He gave Nina some applause. She bowed playfully.

"It may take a while for me to show you those moves step by step, so you can just rinse off the chicken or the asparagus for now."

"I'll do the asparagus."

He showed her where to snap them. He then seasoned the whole chicken and massaged all the fine spices into the skin. Nina was glad she didn't have to do that part. She thought it would've made a mess of her nails, for sure. She planned to take a purposely long time with the asparagus.

"You look really nice tonight. Anybody ever tell you that you look like Nia Long with different eyes? You practically have the same names." He turned the bird over and began cutting it up.

"Nah," Nina said, shaking her head as she snapped the green stems. "She is way more beautiful."

"*You're* beautiful, especially with your almond-shaped eyes and sexy mouth. I think you look better than Nia."

"Thank you," Nina said, but thought he was sniffing a little too much off the spice rack.

He cut up the chicken expertly and seasoned the pan. "Why don't you think you're beautiful?"

Nina never classified herself as a beauty, and no one thought she was but her dead father. To hear Lamont say it made her think that maybe she was beautiful, at least to him, and that was enough. "I think you can help me get used to it. I never really saw myself that way. Just unique."

He smiled at her. "We're gonna have a long talk tonight, Nina."

When she was done rinsing the stems, she placed them in another pan. He handed her seasoning for the rice that she poured into the boiling water. It was a simple dinner and she was glad he was managing the major components. As she watched him prepare the chicken, he explained how he cut it and what seasonings worked best with poultry. And he didn't even mention Frank's Hot Sauce, the only "seasoning" Trent liked. He made sure there was enough water in the pot for the rice and explained how rice needed to be cooked. Too much water and it's soggy and too little water and it's hard. Who knew, Nina thought.

He let Nina off the hook as he meddled some more in the

kitchen. She was free to roam around his place and relax. She admitted to herself that it was fun cooking with him. She had learned a few things already.

Lamont's place was just like she expected. It was different from Ahmasi's laid-back style, and from her nonexistent style back home. The first time she was here, she couldn't see as much because the lights were dimmed. Until today, she never really had a moment to snoop around. Lamont had everything meticulously placed as if he were preparing for a shoot for *Town & Country*. Slim, white, rectangular-shaped couches lined the wall of the apartment. The material was a soft suede that looked warm, but modern. It made his oak floors stand out and gave the room a spacious feel. Nina ran her hands down the hundreds of books in a cherry-stained bookcase. There were lots of philosophy books and computer manuals. A white and red throw rug sat in the center, but it looked like some kind of sheepskin. She loved it. She wanted to roll all around in it.

She crept into his bedroom. As she walked around, he was shouting out some stuff about his home and how it needed to be tidied up. *If this place was any cleaner, I would suggest we eat off the floor.* It looked like it was barely lived in. His bedroom was the same. That she remembered vaguely from last time. His bed had a solid oak headboard, and it looked expensive and well crafted. All the edges of his dark coffee-colored bedspread were tucked in. There wasn't even a crease, she noticed. The sound of pans and pots rattled all the way down the hall. She wasn't convinced that a man could keep his place so tight as this. She poked around some more.

She opened his closet, and to no surprise, everything was coordinated by color, size, and type. He even had labels on his hangers. His shoes were all in a row. There wasn't a speck of dust.

Nina pulled out his nightstand drawer. She was hoping to find something real, like photos, condoms, some notes, and maybe even a dust ball. Nothing. She slid open his other nightstand drawer. Empty. She noticed that his phone was blinking a light for messages. She pressed the button to check the calls that came in. There were only two. One of them was a female. She was relieved for some reason. She thought maybe he was normal after all. But that relief quickly turned to doubt. She checked again and kept pressing the button. The woman's name kept popping up.

About twenty minutes later, the smell led her back to the living room. "Something smells divine," she said as she admired the way he set the table. It was candlelight with lemon leaves on top of white linen. There were several glasses and a few beautiful, brightly colored bowls.

Nina sat down at the table as he brought the food out. "What do you think of my place?" he asked, holding a steaming dish of chicken by both ends with a pot holder.

"Really nice. Everything is so neat and clean," Nina said as she helped him put the chicken on the table.

"I'm hardly home. That's why. I bought this brownstone like three years ago and I still can't enjoy it. But I sure enjoy the rents my tenants pay," he said, smiling.

Nina thought the two white neighbors downstairs couldn't be family.

As soon as he was done doing his thing, he sat down across from her. They prayed and dug in. Nina had to pace herself. She was starving, and the food was delectable. She noted that the asparagus was just as tasty as the chicken.

"The chicken is delightful," Nina said, admiring the sherry taste and spices. "How do you like the asparagus?"

"Nice and crisp. The rice came out good, too. Firm, just how I like it."

"Where did you learn to cook like this?" she asked.

"My ex-wife. She was good."

Then something occurred to Nina. "What's her name?"

"Emily."

"Oh." Nina nodded. It wasn't who she thought it was. *Good.*

He poured them some wine. One white, one red, in their respective glasses. "You're already spoiling me, Lamont," Nina said.

"You appreciate this. Most women forget what it is to feel like a lady these days," he said sadly.

Then her cell phone beeped.

"Excuse me," she said, pushing out of her chair. It was Trent and she had three missed calls from Ahmasi.

"Sorry," Nina said as she came back to the table.

"Mind if I ask who that was?" His eyebrows connected as his forehead tightened.

"My ex-husband and a friend."

"How is the ex-husband thing going?" He cut his eyes back to his plate.

Nina stuffed rice in her mouth. "My divorce is official. I'm officially a statistic."

"Hey, we can change that right now," he said with a wink.

"You liked being married?" Nina asked.

"I loved it. I mean with the right person it could be magical. But I have to keep my expectations in check. I get a little ahead of myself, sometimes."

"I do, too," she said, but she wanted to get ahead with him. "You seem like the type who wouldn't have a problem getting any woman." Nina helped herself to some more asparagus.

He dug his elbows into the glass table. "I'm just a very serious man, Nina. When you mess with a man like me, you don't have a boyfriend, you have a husband. I demand a lot, and expect a lot."

He continued. "And I like you. I may even want to be with you on a serious level."

He was no joke, Nina thought. He was as serious as she wanted him to be. Anything with him would be real. It was exactly what she wanted to hear. But she wasn't going to be that quick to jump.

"Who is Ansley Jones?" she asked.

Lamont answered quickly, "That's a friend."

Nina stopped chewing. It sounded like more than a friend to Nina. He wiped his mouth roughly with his napkin and scrunched it up in his hands. "But that can be over, if you say the word."

"What word?"

"That you'd be my woman."

Nina understood that she had no right to tell him who to see because they hadn't established anything official until this point. But she realized that he wasn't going to be around forever, either.

"Can we at least start by knowing what the other one likes for breakfast?" Nina said, nursing her glass of red wine.

fifteen

Nina slept on Lamont's chest all night. She adjusted her eyes to the sunlight coming through the bay windows. This was peace. This was all she wanted to end a beautiful evening. She liked Lamont and she wasn't very happy about this Ansley woman, whoever she was. Lamont made it sound cut and dry, but Nina understood women. They were not very good at sharing. Nina never was a child and never would be. She thought about how her life could change in a blink of an eye. She looked at his fine wood furnishings, his Rolex dangling off the nightstand, and his shiny, black Italian loafers across the room. If someone had showed her this picture, she would never had imagined herself in it. But she deserved this, she thought, after everything she had been through. Her mind was still rattled about why Trent and Ahmasi called. She didn't plan on calling them because they were like yesterday's newspapers—irrelevant. This morning was all about Lamont, and she didn't want to go messing that up. She buried herself under the covers until Lamont returned from getting the breakfast.

Lamont walked in with a plastic bag full of delicious smells. She wrapped his gray, soft bedsheets around her and walked out to the living room. She peeked in each bag and saw plates of banana pancakes, sausages, bacon, and fruit salad. She didn't know whether to start on him or on the food first. He was looking good with his morning scruffy face, beige Dockers-style slacks, and a plain white T-shirt and sandals.

She could think of five things she could do with the fruit salad and it wasn't for breakfast. She wanted Lamont and couldn't wait any longer. He didn't sweat her over not having sex yet and nothing turned her on more.

She took a piece of pineapple and popped it in his mouth. He chewed, swallowed, and she kissed the sweetness on his tongue. She dropped the sheet around her to the ground, standing buck naked in his arms.

"Wanna go lay down?" she asked, sliding his hand up and down her body. "I'm much hungrier after exercise."

His eyes got that dreamy look. "I thought you would never ask," he said as Nina grabbed his hand and pulled him into the bedroom, where she removed his clothes, piece by piece. She didn't know whether it was finding out about Ansley or just being in his beautiful home, but she felt something take over her. It wasn't the lust she shared with Ahmasi, but a deep needing feeling that she wanted to give herself to him completely.

"I love your body," Nina said, referring to his built chest, flat stomach, and wide, sculpted shoulders.

"I love—"

Nina put a finger across his lips. "Shhh." She kissed and teased him with her tongue around his neck and chest. The ringlets of black, shiny hairs tickled her nose as she inhaled his scent. She loved a man who smelled like one and felt as good.

"I love the way you make me feel," he said in a deep, throaty voice.

Nina climbed on top of him, but he flipped her over slowly and sucked her nipples until they were raw and sensitive. He traced his tongue down to her belly button. *Please go down, please.* She arched her back slightly as he skipped down to her thighs. She thought by his conservative nature that he didn't go down on women. At this point, she wanted to scream. But then he came back up. His eyes were half-closed and he nibbled the corner of her thigh, moving higher and higher. She thought he shouldn't have any trouble finding her spot because she had a Brazilian. Her clit was like, "Hello, this way, please."

Lamont seemed to enjoy that her entire pussy was staring him in the face. He planted deep, big-lipped kisses on her pussy. The vibrating motions from his lips made her moan.

With the tip of his tongue, as light as a feather, he licked the inside of her lips, starting from the top and working his way down to the bottom. He sucked lovingly on her clit, making it knot up so much it hurt. She gripped the sheets to stay composed. Opening his mouth wide, he sucked her entire pussy until she collapsed her legs beside him. She was surprised that he was as uninhibited as he was, or maybe he was just glad the time had come. He lifted her legs and threw them over his shoulders like a champ. He was sucking on her like she wasn't a person with a face. As if she was just a piece of meat. And she was ready to be simmered and cooked.

"Hey, Nina, I got some peach cobbler today," Ms. Bauer said as she waved at Nina from her top-floor window.

Nina waved back. "I'll be up in a few," Nina said as she disappeared into her apartment. She didn't want to be rude to Ms.

Bauer, but she wasn't hungry after the breakfast she and Lamont had finally gotten around to eating. But she figured a few bites wouldn't hurt. She actually had gained back her ten pounds since being in New York, and it wasn't going to all the right places. Nina tucked her stomach in and out in the mirror. She was carrying around a little pouch and smiled at the thought that Ms. Bauer might start assuming she was pregnant.

Nina knocked lightly on Ms. Bauer's door, but it was already open.

Ms. Bauer had on a summery red and pink housedress that complemented her light brown skin and rosy cheeks. She set down two places of sliced peach cobbler with a dollop of whipped cream.

"Sit down, child. I just came from Sunday church service and I usually like to have something sweet to eat afterward," Ms. Bauer said, pulling out a chair. "Don't stand there like the food is gonna jump in your mouth."

Nina sat down and commenced to dig in.

"How is things?" Ms. Bauer asked, sitting across from her with a tender look in her eyes.

"They are okay. Just enjoying the city."

"How is you and that boy on the bike?"

"I stopped seeing him," Nina said, relishing the flavor of the pie. She didn't know why she was revealing her business to Ms. Bauer, but the pie sure made it easier. She appreciated Ms. Bauer looking out for her; without Dee, she missed having someone older to talk to. She was getting used to Ms. Bauer's food, too. "I think I found a good man. He's so handsome, kind, and he lives in Brooklyn, too."

"Does he ride a bike?" she asked with a frown.

"No, Ms. Bauer," Nina said with a smile. "He is also very patient with me."

"Well, I don't wanna be in your business. But I knew there was something about that one on the bike. There was a look to him that didn't sit right in my spirit. He look like he got a lot of secrets."

"We all do, Ms. Bauer."

"So what's this new guy's name?"

"Lamont."

"Now that's a real name for a man—" Ms. Bauer's phone rang, so she excused herself.

Nina ate some more, not leaving a crumb on the plate.

"Nina, honey, it's Dee."

"Tell her to call me downstairs," Nina said as she rose to leave.

Ms. Bauer hung up the phone. "She said she been trying to reach you all night last night."

"I hope everything's all right."

"You weren't home last night?"

"Ms. Bauer, let me go before I miss her call again. Thanks again for the pie!" Nina said, running down the steps when she heard the phone ring.

She belted through the door and picked it up. "Hey, girl—"

"Trent is dead!" Dee screamed through the phone.

Nina's heart stopped.

"Nina? Nina?"

Nina hung up the phone and stood still like she was frozen in time.

sixteen

By the end of the day on Monday, Nina was a basket case. She was avoiding everyone's calls until she could process exactly what was happening. She slept like a baby last night, but this morning it all hit her like a ton of bricks. As much as she despised Trent, she wouldn't wish death on anybody. On top of that, Delores was giving her the cold shoulder today and Nina thought that she was just going to make her suffer until she fired her. Nina was doing her best to avoid that day; she felt if Delores could see how dedicated she was to her job then maybe she'd reconsider. That was why she didn't call in this morning, but it was only her body that showed up. No one could tell what she was going through because she was good at playing the role. But she had a nagging feeling that she was responsible for what happened to Trent. The thought of Ahmasi and his involvement tiptoed through her mind, but she was aware that it could be anything because Trent was involved in a million things.

After lunch, Nina caught Melanie tending to her swollen red

eye in the mirror. Melanie spread ointment on it to cover up the puffiness and squirted some eye drops to get rid of the redness.

"What happened to you?" Nina asked.

"Pablo slapped me up last night. It's no big deal," Melanie said angrily, dabbing some concealer over her eyelid to blend away the redness.

Nina thought that by her tone she didn't want Nina to start preaching. It sounded like Melanie had heard it many times before. If any man ever hit her, Nina thought, she would let everyone know, including the police. She didn't understand women like Melanie.

"Can you stop looking at me like that?" Melanie asked with a nervous laugh. "Things got heated last night."

"Over Javier?"

"I don't even remember after he knocked me so hard in the head. It was probably Javier," Melanie said matter-of-factly.

"Melanie, what he did to you isn't cool. Did you call the cops?" Nina said, examining the side of Melanie's face that had small scratches.

Melanie gently took her hand away. "Please, I don't need any more drama or lectures. This is how Pablo and I have always been."

They both looked in the mirror until Melanie broke down. "I'm so embarrassed. I don't know what got into him last night."

Nina put her arms around Melanie. At a time when she needed support, someone else needed it just as bad. "You have my number; you can always call me if you need a place to stay."

"It's okay, I usually go to my mother's house," Melanie said, holding back sniffles. She ran her hands through her short-cropped hair and her red-painted lips spread from ear to ear. "Okay, okay, that's enough. I'm always crying," she said, half laughing with tears flowing down.

Nina held her by her shoulders until she calmed down. "Go home."

"I can't, I have too many clients today. But look, enough about me. How was your weekend?"

Nina could only think of what happened to Trent. "My ex-husband was killed."

Melanie threw her hand over her mouth. "Oh, my God!"

Nina gave her a look to keep it down. "I don't know all the details, but I feel horrible. I'm wondering if there was anything I missed."

"Things happen," Melanie said, carefully moving Nina's stray hair strands from her face. "And they happen for a reason. I'm sure you'll find out."

"That's what I'm afraid of," Nina said, putting her arms around herself.

"Sometimes I wish Pablo would drop dead so I could be with Javier." Melanie spoke softly, looking up at the ceiling.

Nina's shoulders shuddered at the iciness of Melanie's words. The hate in her voice for her husband Pablo disturbed Nina. She didn't feel that kind of hate for Trent and it made her feel a little better.

When Nina returned home that evening, she expected to see Ms. Bauer and she was relieved she didn't. She spoke to Lamont for a little while to assure him things were fine at work, but she also told him she wasn't feeling well and was going to bed early. He seemed like he wasn't convinced, and she promised to call him after she spoke to Dee.

"Sorry about yesterday," Nina said at the sound of Dee's voice.

"Girl, please, I understand. I realize I kind of dropped it on you like a bomb. I apologize."

"There's no good way to deliver that kind of news, Dee. But I want to know what the hell happened." Nina sat down on the edge of her bed.

"From what I heard, that guy Ahmasi was down here this weekend. A few people saw them together and we both know Trent owed him money."

Nina chewed on her thumb as she thought deeply about Ahmasi. "Are you saying Ahmasi killed him?"

"Yes, I am. We know Trent was up to no good, but he was really just a dumb-ass country boy. His schemes are not at the level of those New York guys. They found Trent's body by the creek, with eighteen bullet wounds."

"Spare me the details, Dee."

"I'm not telling you this for my health. The police can't find Ahmasi and nobody's talking. I'm just saying you need to watch your back."

"I have one question," Nina said as she took in a full, long breath. "Did Trent ever pay him back?"

"No."

Nina imagined that was the reason why Ahmasi may have done what he did.

"Nina, don't go playing detective. If that Negro comes near you, call the police. Or better yet, run."

Nina was definitely worried, but she didn't see Ahmasi killing anyone. "How badly does Ahmasi need that money that he would kill for it?" Nina asked.

"Enough that he may even come to you for it. Maybe you should come home, Nina."

"Oh, hell, no. I am not coming home ever. I'll be all right."

"Promise me you will stay away from that man. He is dangerous."

"I promise," Nina said, but she knew eventually Ahmasi would call again.

At around 5 A.M., her cell phone beeped and it was Ahmasi.

"I need you to meet me in front of Tommy's Coffee Shop on Eighty-sixth Street in an hour," the message said. Nina's instinct told her to call the cops, but she had no proof that he killed Trent. She wanted to hear the story and they were meeting in a public place that gave her no reason not to go. She hurried and got herself together on the humid, rainy April morning. This was something she had to do for her own peace of mind.

An hour and fifteen minutes later, a cold hand tapped her shoulder. She spun around and Ahmasi was standing there with a bushel of daisies.

"Let's get on the bike and go for a ride," he said, handing her a helmet. "I missed you."

"No, no," Nina said, waving her finger back and forth. "We can talk right here. I ain't going anywhere with you." Nina grabbed the flowers from him and put them in the garbage. "What the hell do you want from me?" she asked as they walked in the coffee shop and sat down.

He gave a sarcastic smirk. "I guess you heard what happened to your ex-husband."

"I sure did, and I don't want to have anything to do with it," Nina said as they both sat on the stools overlooking the busy street.

"Coffee?" the red-haired waitress asked, but Nina and Ahmasi ignored her, and she walked away.

"You have everything to do with it!" he spat back. "You told me that motherfucker was gonna give me my money."

"Look, I don't know what I said, but that is between you and Trent. Why did you kill him?"

"What?" he asked, repulsed at her accusation.

Nina straightened out her back. She hadn't expected that reaction. "You heard what I said."

"I didn't kill anyone," Ahmasi said, disregarding her comment like a joke. "I would never do that."

It scared Nina that she believed him. "Then why are people saying that?"

"Maybe because they saw me in Houston, a new face, and we was hanging together."

Nina threw her hands up in the air. "Why were you in Houston? Were you going to get the money?"

Ahmasi paused and drank the glass of water on the table. "I don't know why I was going; I guess I needed to get away after you broke up with me and decided I might as well get my money while I had the chance."

"So what happened when you were there?"

Ahmasi turned away, and he held his head down. "We was all drinking at the pool hall, and I asked Trent for the money. He said he didn't have it. That he promised to get it to me. I got tired of hearing that for two years. I felt I was being played. So we started fighting." He stopped for a moment to collect his thoughts. "Then he said you had the money and you were supposed to pay me back."

"Me?"

"Then he started calling you all kind of whore and bitch names. I lost it and kicked his ass. A few of my boys got in and we beat him down."

Nina's stomach felt weak. She could just envision Trent bleeding and helpless.

"We left him in the alleyway and I don't know what happened after that. He was alive when we left."

"But they found him in the creek."

He shrugged his shoulders. "Maybe someone else took him there."

Nina composed herself. She wanted to get out of that coffeehouse as fast as she could. "I heard enough," she said, shaking her head. "Please, just forget you ever met me. Don't contact me or anything. Or I'll call the police."

"Call the police for what?" he said with a look of hate all over his face. "They questioned me already and let me go. You better check where you getting your info from."

Nina got up to leave and he jerked her arm back down. "Sit down," he demanded.

"Don't fucking ever touch me!" Nina yelled at him and knocked his hand off her. Her voice alarmed the other diners who looked on. "I don't know about you, but *I* will smoke your ass."

Ahmasi laughed lightly. "Fine, go ahead then. But I want my money, Nina."

Nina dashed out of the diner, and realized that maybe she should've stayed in bed this morning.

seventeen

A month and a half had passed before Nina heard anything else about Trent's death. Lamont accompanied her to the funeral, where the critical eyes of her relatives and mother looked on. She stayed only for a few days. Dee wasn't in town because she had another business convention to attend, but she had been there for Nina so many times before. Now Nina had a man in her life, who cared for her and protected her every interest. Lamont also joined her as she visited her father's grave; she didn't know when the next time would be. Everything else in Houston represented everything she wanted to forget.

"That looks good on you," Lamont said about Nina's classy gold and green summer wrap dress. They stood on his mother's doorstep on a tree-lined block in middle-class Riverdale on Saturday. Lamont had invited Nina to his mother's house for dinner.

Nina wondered if she looked good enough. She thought maybe she should've bought some pearls in case his mother was as conservative as Lamont. Nina pictured his mother to be an elegant and statuesque woman.

Instantly the door swung open. "My, my, my. It's about time you visited the woman who birthed you," Lamont's mother said, arms wide open. Lamont leaned into her embrace.

"This is Nina. Nina, this is my mom, Mrs. Franklin. . . ."

She gave Nina one staunch look, then a closemouthed smile. "Welcome, dear," she said, ushering them inside.

Nina thought she looked exactly like she imagined. She was a light-skinned woman with a perfectly groomed coif and eyelashes that went on for days. She wore pearls with her simple peach-colored slacks and matching embroidered blouse. Nina kicked herself for not wearing pearls.

They entered her living room, which was a lot like Lamont's. Everything was in its place—minimal, dark, cherrywood furnishings. She lived alone and it showed.

"Mrs. Franklin, you have a really nice view from your window," Nina said, admiring the trees and the water view. "It reminds me of where I grew up."

"Mom, Nina is from Houston," Lamont said, like it was the most exotic place on earth. Nina sat down next to him and began to feel uneasy.

Mrs. Franklin batted her eyelashes repeatedly as if she were trying to fight off the distasteful look on her face. "Well, that is very nice. I spent some time in Houston. Care for a drink?"

Lamont and Nina nodded as she went to the kitchen. He kissed Nina's neck playfully and said, "I think she likes you." But Nina wasn't as sure.

Mrs. Franklin returned with a pitcher of ice-cold lemonade and glasses. She served each of them a glass.

"My mother was a nurse. She worked at some big Houston hospital," Lamont went on. "I think it was—"

"It was Mount Cedar. That was my first ever hospital job. I only worked there a year."

"Were you born in Houston?" Nina asked.

"I was born in Louisiana. Houston was one of the closest big cities."

"I didn't live in the big city part at all," Nina said. "I'm a small-town country girl. At least I was."

Lamont shot Nina a pleasing look.

"Once a country girl, always a country girl." Mrs. Franklin's defined eyebrows rose up to her forehead. "I'm going to check on the lamb chops. Dinner should be ready in a few."

Nina waited until she was gone before she said to Lamont, "Why didn't you tell me your mom worked in Houston?"

"I forgot," he said, sipping his lemonade and beaming with a smile. She couldn't help but think how fine he looked today with his white linen slacks and shirt that swathed his thick, muscular body. She wanted Mrs. Franklin to like her.

Mrs. Franklin ordered them around the table as she laid down a tray of lamb chops, grilled asparagus, rice, and a fresh field greens salad with sweet corn. By the look of everything, this was where Lamont had gotten his kitchen skills from, Nina thought.

"Where exactly are you from in Houston?" Mrs. Franklin asked a few minutes into dinner.

Nina quietly put down her fork and looked at Lamont. "It's a small town, you probably wouldn't know it."

Mrs. Franklin's eyes grew. "Try me," she said coolly.

Lamont sprinkled some balsamic dressing on his salad and gave his mom a look. There was too much unspoken stuff going on, and it was making Nina nervous as hell. Nina said, "It's a town called Allswell."

Mrs. Franklin chewed her salad, absorbed in thought.

"This lamb is so tender. I could eat these alone," Lamont said, taking another one.

Nina agreed. "I gotta learn how to make this."

"A country girl who can't cook?" Mrs. Franklin commented.

Nina didn't think she was trying to be funny, either.

"Nina is a massage therapist. My mom's had arthritis for years, and I've been trying to get her to come to you."

"Is that right, Mrs. Franklin. You know, a couple of sessions of—"

Just when she thought she had forgotten, Mrs. Franklin said, "Ahh, now I remember. Allswell. I knew a gentleman from there."

"Really?" Nina said, the lamb now feeling like rubber as she tried to swallow. Her town was small, so anyone Mrs. Franklin knew, she had to know, too.

"Sweetheart, I think I know you and your family."

Lamont looked at Nina like that was supposed to be good. Nina wasn't sure where Mrs. Franklin was taking this. Nina felt naked all of a sudden. She thought Mrs. Franklin would want to know what her polished, conservative son was doing with a girl like her.

"Uh, Mrs. Franklin, I doubt it. My family is very small." Nina politely signaled for her to pass the dressing.

She did. "Was your father named Errol?"

Nina laid down her fork, but didn't look up. "Why?"

"Because I was seeing a gentleman at that time who used to bring this little girl named Nina around." Her eyes lowered on Nina.

"There could be lots of Ninas," Lamont said, putting a wedge between the tension. "And if it is Nina, what's your point?"

"Nothing," Mrs. Franklin said, changing back to her "nice" voice. "I was just thinking what a small world."

◆ ◆ ◆

Nina helped Mrs. Franklin in the kitchen and cleared the table. Mrs. Franklin didn't offer, but Nina was pining for some alone time. Lamont seemed cool, but he too was a little annoyed by his mother's brashness. Nina didn't know what was up with the two of them, but Lamont was clearly the kinder, happier one.

"So, Nina, what do you think of my son?" Mrs. Franklin asked as they placed the dishes in the dishwasher.

"You raised a good son, Mrs. Franklin. When I came to New York, I hardly knew anyone. He's been good to me."

She slammed the dishwasher door and turned to Nina. "Let's stop playing games here. I knew your family, especially your father." Mrs. Franklin's eyes grew again. She had big Diana Ross eyes that looked half-closed most of the time.

Nina lost her breath. From the look on Mrs. Franklin's face, Nina could tell something awful had happened to Mrs. Franklin and it was her family's fault. Now it would become hers.

"What do you want with my son?"

"I don't know what happened to you, Mrs. Franklin, but Lamont and I are just fine. I don't have anything to do with it."

"Lamont can't possibly be fine with you if he knew all about your background. Does he?" she asked, her voice louder as she clutched her pearl necklace. "You must have done something to him."

"What are you talking about?" Nina asked, utterly confused. She thought Mrs. Franklin was delirious and maybe had forgotten to take her medication. She was beginning to feel like Mrs. Franklin was setting her up to look bad for no reason.

"I know how you country girls get your men. You use all kinds of tricks of the trade. What have you done?"

"Listen, Mrs. Franklin, I don't know what you have against me. I didn't do anything to Lamont that he didn't enjoy as much as I did. And I'm not really appreciating your tone when you don't even know me."

"I know you," she said, batting her eyelashes violently. "I was your father's mistress for seven years. Remember Lady Ann?"

Nina's stomach knotted up. She put her hand over it and took a seat. Lady Ann was one of her daddy's main ladies. He used to take Nina with him to go see her. She always remembered her being mean-looking, but she made the best bread pudding Nina ever tasted. Lady Ann's name was mentioned a lot by Nina's mother, mostly in a screaming rage at her daddy. Nina didn't know everything that happened, but she remembered her daddy feeling up on Lady Ann when he visited her. They'd disappear in the back room while Nina watched television with her teenaged son, who had to be Lamont. He'd always be buried in some schoolbook, blatantly ignoring and bothered by his mother's actions. Nina's father used to say she was giving him his medicine since she was a nurse. Nina had been eight and didn't give it a second thought. But Lamont was fifteen and knew exactly what was going down. But what blew Nina's mind the most was that it was rumored that Lady Ann was the one who "fixed" her father.

Mrs. Franklin moved toward Nina in measured steps. "I loved your father till this very day, but that man destroyed me. Your mother drove me out of town with nothing except the clothes on my back and my son. That woman did something to me and I never been the same. And your father let it happen."

"I don't know what happened between you and my mama and my father. I really don't have anything to do with that—"

"You have everything to do with it!" she shouted. "If it wasn't for you I would have been married to him and not living this miserable life. He would have done anything for you. Just for you! That's why I'm glad he's alone like I've been all these years. But at least I get visitors."

Nina was about to say something, when Lamont walked in the room.

"What the hell is going on with you two?" Lamont asked, storming into the kitchen with the TV remote in his hand.

Tears welled up in Nina's eyes. It was like everywhere she went her past was there, too. "I gotta go," Nina said, rushing past Lamont and grabbing her bag.

"Hold on," Lamont said, coming after her, while his mother shouted curse words behind her.

Nina wanted to throw up anything that woman had prepared for her. She was sick to her stomach, but she couldn't leave. Lamont was blocking the door.

"Nobody is going anywhere until I know what happened."

"This woman—" Mrs. Franklin huffed, standing behind Lamont "—is just like her father: dirty, conniving, and her family is a bunch of incestuous pigs. Did she tell you how she fucked her stepfather?"

Nina had had enough. She stepped to Mrs. Franklin as Lamont stood between them. "You don't know what happened to me and I can deal with that. But with all due respect, Mrs. Franklin, I won't let you degrade my daddy's name. I may not be perfect, beautiful, or even honest, but I am my father's daughter. I won't stand for it," Nina said, making sure to maintain her composure and dignity, unlike Mrs. Franklin.

"Your father ruined me. I lost my job at the hospital and any sense of integrity I had. I gave him all my money and my love, only to have him stay with his family because of a runny-nosed, nappy-haired twit like you."

Nina was burning up. She wanted to pelt Mrs. Franklin a quick fast one across the mouth, but she felt defeated, weak.

"I think this is a good time to leave," Lamont said, taking Nina by the arm. He gave his mother, who stood there surprised, an icy glare as if she expected them to stay for dessert.

"I don't want to see that girl again!" she shouted as Lamont and Nina walked out.

"Then you probably won't see me again," Lamont said as he slammed the door.

Nina prepared to be bombarded with questions and doubt on the way back to Brooklyn. But she wasn't. Lamont knew eventually he'd be able to get the whole story. She was embarrassed for herself and for Lamont. As they drove down the Henry Hudson Parkway, Nina said, "I'm really sorry if I was in any way disrespectful to your mother. But I—"

"It's fine, Nina. My mother has often been known for lashing out like that. I've always remembered her as a really unhappy woman. But now I know why." He broke a sad smile. "I knew there was something familiar about you."

"I'm just glad we're not related," Nina said as she looked at the cars zooming by beside him.

"I couldn't believe she was talking to you like that. She should've confided in me first."

Nina dried her eyes with Kleenex. "I'm just tired of hurting. I could've stayed in Houston for that."

They stopped at a red light and he caressed Nina's wet face. "I won't let anyone mistreat you, Nina. I love you." He wiped a tear away. "You can stop hurting now."

eighteen

Nina told Lamont she needed some time to herself after the episode at his mother's house last week. It was Memorial Day weekend, and she was spending it alone. She wanted to clear her mind and get grounded again. As much as Lamont tried to act like it didn't bother him, she could sense that he had lots of questions and his image of her was stained. She imagined the awful things his mother had said about her family to him over the years. Mrs. Franklin wasn't the type to forgive and forget and she wasn't out for payback, but back pay.

But what bothered her most was that here she was in a new city, with the same feelings she had always struggled with. She had a good man in her life for a change, and that was being threatened before they could even hit their stride. Maybe she just wasn't the kind of woman mothers liked, she thought. Her mother hated her, and now Mrs. Franklin did, too. Ms. Bauer wasn't a mother and she got along fine with her when she wasn't being too nosy. Again, it came down to Dee being still the only person she believed had her back. But they were both growing. Dee had her business, her husband, and her children; Nina had very little in comparison. She wanted to have it all but, she thought, maybe she was looking to another to do it for her. She needed to get her own, and it just wasn't about getting a man. She wanted her own identity, but at the same time, she loved being Lamont's woman. She could see her future in his eyes. But this weekend proved how quickly that could change, too.

When the phone rang, Nina dried her eyes.

"This is Nina," she said, not recognizing Dee's number on the Caller ID.

"How are you?" Dee asked.

The background noise on Dee's end was almost unbearable. Nina struggled to hear. "Where are you?"

"I'm at the airport in Chicago waiting for my flight back home. So what's been happening?"

"Too much, too soon," Nina said, falling back on the bed. She was still in her nightgown.

"Did you see that crazy fool?"

"Yes, and he told me he didn't kill Trent. He said he beat him up."

"Kill, beat up. What's the difference? He was involved."

"I know, but he told me the cops let him go after they talked to him."

"Whatever. Those types of men are professionals; they will never give you the straight story. I heard the cops let him go, and I was shocked."

"I'm not even sure he killed him, but I am sure that he is crazy. I met up with him and told him to not ever contact me again or else."

"You are bold, girl. I would've played friends, told him I got a job offer in Croatia and I'm leaving for good. You can't irritate men like that."

Nina thought back to the moment at the coffee shop a few weeks ago and remembered how irritated Ahmasi really had been. "He told me Trent told him I had the money."

"Now that's cold. How could Trent let you take the fall for him? He lied on his deathbed?"

"You damn right, he lied. I don't got ten Gs to give to anyone. Now the problem is mine."

Dee and Nina remained silent for a few seconds.

"I can give you the money so he can leave you alone," Dee said suddenly.

"Hell, no, Dee. Fuck Ahmasi. Besides, I think he was just saying that to mess with me. I know he can't stand that I broke up with him."

"All right, Nina, my flight is about to board. But remember, please stay as far away as possible from him. That Negro is up to something."

"Later, Dee."

After she hung up, Nina double-checked that her front door was locked when she heard the zoom of a motorcycle speeding down her street. Dee was making her extra worried, which made her feel there was so much more to the story she didn't know and she didn't want to know.

When Nina returned to work on Tuesday, she was feeling much better. She and Lamont had communicated via text this weekend and she appreciated that. He gave her the room she needed, but she knew the time would come when he'd need his own room and she wasn't always very good at that. She couldn't wait to see him after work. As she walked the halls, she looked for Melanie, and realized that she wouldn't get back from vacation until the end of the week. She wondered how things were going. The spa was quiet since Delores warned it would be a slow week. The trickling water from the waterfall in the reception area was the only thing she could hear. She had only three clients today, which meant it was going to be a short one.

Delores poked her head into the employee locker room. "Nina, would you mind coming into my office, please?"

"Sure, I'll be there in two minutes." Nina tied her uniform around her waist.

Nina didn't know why Delores needed to see her, but she hoped it wasn't about Lamont. Weeks had passed since she had seen her at the grocery store. Nina walked down a few doors to Delores's office.

"Nina, close the door, please," Delores said, removing her glasses. "Sit down."

Nina sat down and her knees began to shake a bit. She had been through enough already and didn't need any more surprises. "Is everything okay?"

Delores looked at her face strangely. "How is Mr. Franklin doing?"

"Good," Nina said dryly. "Why do you ask?"

"Nina," Delores said, folding her hands on her desk. "You and Mr. Franklin are obviously an item. I haven't heard from him in weeks. This is what happens when my therapists date clients. We lose the clients. I can't run a business that way."

Nina's shoulders slumped. "He wants to come back, but the two-visit policy—"

"He won't come back. Many clients hook up and get the services for free from their partner or end up elsewhere. Trust me, I had clients that came back, but eventually something happened and I never saw them again. The fact is, you broke company policy."

"Not intentionally, Delores."

"You gave me your word."

"I know, but Lamont and I are very serious. We actually met for the first time years ago and didn't know it," Nina said with an overactive smile.

"You're my most requested therapist, caring and professional. Except for the big error you made after being warned by me." Delores handed Nina a folded piece of paper. "Sorry, but I have to let you go."

Nina read the letter that stated that today was the effective date. "But, Delores, I need this job—"

"I'm sorry, Nina."

"Delores—"

"Please, Nina, let's not make this any more uncomfortable than it already is," she said.

Nina wanted to tell Delores off, but didn't. She walked out of her office and packed her belongings. Though the time was brief, she thought she had learned a lot from Delores that she could use in her future plans. She wrote a brief good-bye note to Melanie and stuck it in her locker.

nineteen

Nina didn't know how she was going to get by without a job. She didn't want to ask Lamont for money, but counted that she had only enough to pay next month's rent. She didn't want to start relying on him like she had with Trent, and borrowing from Dee again didn't seem right. She had to find another job and needed to figure out her next plan.

Being with Lamont couldn't have come at a better time. After work, she trotted down to a hip, swanky restaurant on the Lower East Side. The music was good and so were the vibes, but the menu was sushi. Nina never liked her food raw, and opted for the California rolls, which seemed safe enough, while Lamont ordered a variety of sushi dishes. It was a nice change, she thought, except for the chopsticks.

"Feel better after this weekend?" he asked, sipping his sake.

Nina grabbed her Coke. "Yeah, but I got another problem."

Lamont rolled his eyes. "What now?"

"Delores fired me today," Nina said, wondering if he was already getting tired of her drama.

"Damn," he said as he sipped some more. He signaled the waitress for another.

Nina watched him as he ate the edamame without a care. She expected more of a reaction. "Is that all you have?"

"I can order more," he said, looking for the waitress again.

"No, silly. Not that, I mean, I told you I lost my job. You know exactly why I lost it, too," she said, helplessly battling with her chopsticks. She wanted to throw them at him.

"So it's my fault?"

"You said it, not me."

"Look, I'm not going to get upset about you losing your job. Why do we need two upset people? That won't solve anything."

Nina was frustrated. "Then what do I do? I loved that job and now I have to start over and find something else. I got lucky with Serenity. It was just opening up."

"Who says you have to find another job?" he asked as the young Asian waitress set down their plates.

"I must get another job," Nina said, struggling to grab her rice with the chopsticks. A large clump fell on her jeans.

"I can take care of you. I have no problem doing that until you find a job you absolutely love, like you did Serenity," he said, handling his chopsticks with skill as he moved from plate to plate.

"Lamont, I can't allow that. Thank you, but no thank you," Nina said.

"Let me help you with these chopsticks so you can get some protein in that brain because what I said made perfect sense." He spent a few moments showing Nina how to work the chopsticks with ease. She got it after a couple of tries.

But she didn't thank him this time. She didn't like his tone. She wondered if he was holding some resentment toward her. "Are you upset about your mom still?"

"Not at all," he replied. "Come on, let's eat."

"Wait, I just want you to understand that I can do this on my own. Give me some time to figure out how I can solve my own problem." Nina was firm. She thought she had to draw the line with a man like Lamont because he had a tendency for controlling things. And the only one who was controlling her life was her.

"Fine, work it out, then," Lamont said, like he wanted to forget about the subject. "But if we're going to be a couple, you have to start acting like my woman."

"Now what is that supposed to mean? What have I been acting like?"

Lamont skillfully picked up a slice of ginger with his chopsticks and slipped it between his lips. Though they were both not in the best mood, Lamont still did it for Nina. She knew what they both needed.

"Listen, why don't we work this all out back at your place after this?" Nina asked.

"I was just thinking that," Lamont answered as they took their meals to go.

Nina and Lamont couldn't get their clothes off fast enough. It had been five days since they had been this close. They couldn't wait until they got inside. Lamont's tongue discovered Nina's as they made up for lost time. Lamont picked Nina up and carried her to his bedroom and laid her down like a fine, expensive silk. His lips traveled from her pretty nose to the sweet slope of her plump breasts. He lifted up her lavender cotton tee, freed a breast from her black lace bra, and fed on her nipple. He freed the other breast from the bra, and sucked on that one, too. Nina closed her eyes and gave Lamont total charge of her body. She was in no mood to fuck back. She just wanted to enjoy the array of sensations from Lamont's hands, tongue, and lips.

Before long, she had her legs wrapped around his waist as he penetrated her body with urgency. Nina raised her arms over her head as their hips rocked together, beating the headboard against the wall. Thank God there were no neighbors next door, she thought as Lamont held her hands down on the bed.

"I love you," he whispered over her, his goatee and mustache catching the sweat drizzling down the side of his face.

She wasn't ready to say the words, but she felt them. She licked a line of sweat from his face and found his lips again, sucking his tongue, but thinking about going down, and she did, lovingly holding his length in her mouth until her lips and his dick were one.

They made love for the rest of the hour. Nina was struck by Lamont's passion, and her own. The sex with him was something she had never experienced. It wasn't about getting off, but about another level. Though he was throwing it down, he wouldn't be the brother getting the "freaknasty" award of the year, but maybe runner-up.

Nina played with Lamont's chest hair as they both rested to the tune of the evening's news on television.

"Sorry if I was a little dismissive about the whole job thing," he said, covering her shoulders with the plush, white cotton sheets.

"I knew a taste of this sweet stuff and you'd be back to your old self," she said, stealing a glance at the mirror on his dresser, which reflected back her hair that was matted down and frizzed out. She liked that she didn't have to hide anything real from him and lay back down. He didn't even seem to notice.

"I ain't gonna lie, you did have me hanging out there with no rope. I wasn't sure if you wanted to see me again because of my mother."

The tone of his voice saddened Nina because she didn't want to give him any doubt about her commitment. She understood what men did when they had doubt, like her daddy once had. "Well, I apologize, too. I shouldn't have cut you off like that. It was a little cold."

His lips landed on her cool forehead. "That's exactly what I meant earlier when I said you need to start acting like my woman. I want you to share *everything*."

Nina sighed. She had an idea of what he was referring to, but she wasn't ready yet to reveal it all. "You have to trust me."

"I do or we wouldn't be here."

"You said you loved me, right?"

"And I know you will eventually."

"How do you know I don't already?"

Lamont played with the remote. "Because there's still so much I don't know. Did you have sex with your stepfather?"

Nina turned her back to him. "I was raped," she said quietly, afraid to see his reaction.

"I'm sorry, Nina, but that's something I should know. When was it?"

"Many years ago, okay," Nina said, edging out of bed. "I don't wanna talk about it."

"Fine," he said, feeling torn between asking too much or too little. "I'm not judging you. I just better not ever see that man."

Nina sat on the foot of the bed. "I'll tell you the whole story one day, but my mom kind of went around and changed the story. She was embarrassed that her neighbors would think her boyfriend wanted me more than her. Instead of telling them the truth, she told them I wanted him."

Lamont shook his head in revulsion. "I guess we both have mothers from hell." He tugged on her arm to bring her to him. "Do you love me?"

Nina went back to the safe place between his arm and chest. "I do," she said.

"And your husband. Did you love him?"

"Yes."

"I know you did. I was hurting for you that day at the funeral. Did you ever hear what happened?"

Nina figured she might as well let it all out. "A guy I knew may have killed him, or at least that's the rumor."

"Someone you knew?"

Nina chewed the inside of her mouth.

"Someone you met in New York?"

"Yes," Nina revealed. "A guy I was seeing—"

"An ex-boyfriend?" Lamont slid away from her. "You only been in New York a few months and most of that time was with me."

Nina had just about had it with Lamont's demands. "I wasn't with you the whole time! I met someone before you."

"And you broke up when?"

"We were never an item, it was just friends—"

"Just fucking!"

She watched as Lamont grabbed his boxers and a tee and threw it over his body. He was fuming. She had no idea he could be this jealous.

"Did you say you trusted me?" Nina asked.

He spun around. "How can I when you forget to tell me an

ex-boyfriend killed your husband? So what's that all about? What else should I know?"

Nina threw the covers off her. "You know, this is too much for me right now—"

"Yes, it is," he said, slipping on pants and shoes. "And it's not so much that it's an ex who killed your ex, but it's the fact that I went all the way to Houston with you and you chose to keep that from me. The only reason I could think you would do that is because you're still seeing him. Right?"

"Wrong!" Nina shot back. She knew better than to tell him about the coffee shop meet, the money, or anything else. This temper was a whole new side to him, she thought. But maybe it was warranted. If she wanted a man who was ready to give her his heart, she had to be willing to give him hers.

He lashed back. "I don't think you're ready for what I'm ready for."

"Whatever," Nina murmured as she fought back tears.

He stood at the door holding his keys. "When I get back, I want you gone."

twenty

Lamont did warn her. He told her he wasn't the type to play. He was serious about her in every way and he was holding her to her end of the deal. She wondered why Lamont cared so much. She had disrespected his intelligence and his ability to give by not being honest with him. At the funeral, she didn't think what it could've looked like with Lamont on her arm after Trent probably had told her family she had met a man already in New York and the rumors in town that it was somebody who was an ex-boyfriend of hers who possibly even killed him. Meeting his mother was one thing, but she grasped that he did deserve to know about the situation between Ahmasi and Trent. Lamont made her feel like she was secretly protecting Ahmasi. But she wasn't, she told herself. She just didn't think things would've gotten this far with Lamont so soon. She argued with herself that she should've told Lamont about the reason behind Trent's death right away. And while she was at it, tell Lamont that she'd been in love with him since the day she set sight on his bald, shiny head in the greeting room at the spa. If Lamont didn't want to ever speak to her again, she expected it, because no one in her life was ever really interested in her side of the story.

Sitting in a neighborhood bar, two weeks later, Nina thought how the last time she was at a place like this was months ago—a hole in the wall with low lights and boisterous laughter intertwined in the clouds of smoke. The Teacup Lounge seemed like ancient history now. She didn't know why she ended up at Michelle's, but it was the closest and cheapest bar advertised in the neighborhood and it was the only bar open at 2 P.M. on a Tuesday afternoon.

Nina wasn't much of a drinker, but she needed something to kick her blues about Lamont and taking a shot or two of Bombay Sapphire to the neck was doing it. However, it didn't stop her from circling a few help wanted ads under Temp Work in the newspaper. The money was going and she had just paid the rent for the next month. She couldn't think of a worse time to be apart from Lamont. Even though he did call twice to check if she needed anything, his calls sounded more like a robotic telemarketer doing his duty than a concerned boyfriend. She didn't call him back.

"Good afternoon, can I speak to Ms. James?" Nina asked as she called a temp agency on her list. She put on her best voice despite being a little tipsy.

"This is she," said a high anxiety–sounding woman on the other end.

"Hello, I'm Nina Bettus, and I'm calling about the ad for temps." Nina took a sip of her drink for strength.

"Do you have a résumé?"

Nina racked her brain. Delores had never asked for it and only needed her massage certificate. She probably just got lucky with Delores that day, she thought back. The résumé she had was outdated and Kmart was the last place of employment. "Yes, I do," Nina said, taking another swig to stop her from just hanging up. She realized she had to fake it until she made it.

"What was your last job?"

"I was a receptionist at a spa. Do you have any salons or spas hiring?"

"Only banks and law firms. Actually we prefer that our temps have a financial background."

Financial background? Nina was pretty much lost. She didn't know if she meant education or what. She already knew money wasn't her thing. "I have some background in that or I can learn." But Nina hated office work with a passion.

"We have a few openings for receptionists, typists. And you have done that, right?"

"Yes," Nina lied.

"Can you handle a multiline board of over thirty?"

"Yes," Nina said in a daze. She thought perhaps it was a bad idea to call when her brain was so foggy.

"Bring in your résumé and ID, and I can see you tomorrow at 1:30 P.M."

"Thank you," Nina said as she took the address down and hung up. When she read it, it was barely legible.

She didn't know what she had obligated herself to, but it was time to go back home. A temp job at a bank sounded fine, but she didn't want to veer too far off her professional path because it was where she could be her best. For now, she needed quick, easy cash until another spa came along.

"How much?" Nina said as she searched her purse to pay the bartender, an identical image of Ike Turner. She dug for quarters and coins.

"It's already taken care of." He smiled, sliding her another shot of Bombay Sapphire. "Here you go, from the gentleman over there in the dreads."

Nina barely was able to get a good focus when she looked around the room and saw him. She thought her mind was playing tricks on her. It was Ahmasi.

"You all right?" he asked, walking up to her stool.

Nina threw back the shot and turned away from him.

"I was watching you for a while and you seem really fucked up," he said, leaning against the bar to look at her face. "I was here to drop off some flyers. I'm not here to bother you."

Nina's eyes scanned his face, which was much clearer. He looked the same with his long, shiny black dreads and soulful eyes. His eyebrows were thick and groomed. He had gained about ten to fifteen pounds, and that made him look healthier and fit.

"Ain't you supposed to be at work?" he asked, trying to trigger some response from her.

"I got fired," she finally said. But she wasn't about to have a walk down memory lane with him, and got up to leave. She rose up slowly, holding the edge of the bar, and stumbled forward.

"Whoa, whoa," Ahmasi said, breaking her fall.

"Get off me," Nina slurred as she adjusted her red tank top that had shown most of her flat belly. She motioned for the door.

"Let me help you." Ahmasi took her hand.

Nina shrugged him off hard and marched out of the door into the street.

"Hold up a minute," he called, walking quickly behind her.

Maybe it was the sudden daylight on her face, but she didn't make it but a foot out the door when she found herself bent over a car. She purged out her several drinks on the hood of a sleek, white Mercedes sedan.

"Shit!" Ahmasi said, pulling her off the car and walking her with brisk steps down the street. He wanted to be far away from the Benz, in case the owner was nearby.

Ahmasi grabbed an unopened bottle of water in his backpack and made her wash her mouth out as they stopped at the corner. They were several blocks from her house. She washed her mouth out and drank the bottle down to the last drop. She was feeling better already, but now her head was throbbing.

Ahmasi walked her to her apartment. "Look, we don't have to talk. I just want to make sure you get in your place safe and sound."

"Did I tell you I lost my job?" Nina said, still toasted from her binge.

"Yes, you did. That's messed up. You can do poetry now," he said with a laugh.

"What?" Nina asked.

"You really need to lie down," he urged.

Ahmasi stood by until Nina stumbled around to ready herself for bed.

Nina didn't look at him but once. She barely recognized that he was there. Her mind reasoned that it was Lamont or Ms. Bauer looking after her. She stripped down to her panties and bra and fell flat-faced on her bed.

She heard the front door click closed. When she woke up a couple of hours later there was a perfume scent not her own in the air. It was then she noticed Ahmasi had been there and had gone. He left her a five-thousand-dollar check in an envelope.

In the morning, Nina read the check for the third time. She knocked herself in the head for not being more aware. She would have never accepted money from Ahmasi. It was blood money. It was the money Trent owed him. She was sure of it. But she kept it and slipped it inside her wallet to deposit it in a brand-new savings account. No one had to know, so no one would know, she said to herself.

But that didn't stop her from finding work. She then raced around for her interview at Shelly James Temps on East Forty-second and Madison. The note she had written at the bar wasn't even legible, but after calling information a few times, she pinned down an exact street address. She dug through some unopened boxes and found her résumé. It was wrinkled and had water stains. She made a note to make a copy of it on her way to the salon to get her hair done. She couldn't possibly go anywhere with her ends needing to be trimmed. She wore her simple, off-white summer suit with a skirt and light jacket and matching heels. She hurried, with a cup of morning tea in her hand, out the door with a tinge of excitement.

About three hours later, Nina found herself in the busy reception area waiting to see Ms. James. There were several women who looked like her filling out applications and taking computer tests. Nina knew her résumé was garbage, but she slipped it in her file and answered the application questions as best as she could.

"I hate these places," said a young woman sitting next to her.

Nina smiled politely, but didn't answer.

"They have you sitting around for hours and then tell you they will call you."

"Do they call?" Nina asked as she admired the girl's sharp beige heels and professional beige sheath dress.

"Maybe, like after you call them a hundred times. You have to harass them. That's how they can see you really want it," she said, playing with her long, black, luxurious weave. Her lips were red and stood out harshly from her caramel skin.

"I'm Nina," Nina said as she stuck out her hand. "What's your name?"

"Zohanna," the girl said, shaking Nina's hand firmly. "What time is your appointment?"

"In fifteen minutes."

"Cool, so is mine, so we must be meeting with different people. Where did you work before?"

"I worked at a spa, but things didn't work out. I just need a job like this, until I can find one I really like."

"I hear you. Well, if you need any referrals, I can give you some of the places I been to. But I have to move around to keep constantly working," Zohanna said as they both heard another name called.

"What do you do?"

"You don't even wanna know," said the girl as she made a devilish grin.

"Try me," Nina said, totally intrigued.

"I danced, you know, pole dancing."

"You were a stripper?"

Zohanna laughed. "Yeah, I was trying to clean it up but it is what it is, I guess."

"Career change?"

"Definitely. Ooh, there goes my name. Listen, how about we meet in like half an hour at the Starbucks downstairs so I can give you the info about the other agencies."

"Cool, thank you," Nina said as Zohanna disappeared behind the glass doors for her interview.

"Nina Bettus," called a short, gray-haired woman with glasses. "Come with me."

Nina followed the older woman through the glass doors, and

felt like she was going in for a physical exam. Nina told herself that if she kept smiling things wouldn't look so bad to Mrs. James. She knew that without putting her best self forward, she would have no chance at getting a job with no skills.

"Hi!" the woman said, magically getting a burst of energy from thin air. "How are you? I'm Shelly James."

"Fine, thank you," Nina said as she took a seat.

"As I looked over your scores and your résumé, I really think you should consider taking some career training classes. Your computer skills are too low and Kmart doesn't exactly make the kind of impression we're looking for," she said, lowering her glasses to the tip of her nose.

"I need a job, Mrs. James, and I can do anything. I don't have time to train; I need to make money."

"Tell me about the last job," Mrs. James said, removing her glasses and taking notes as Nina spoke. Nina explained all the duties, including embellishing her "receptionist" duties to make an impact on Mrs. James.

"Well, why isn't that job on the résumé?" she asked, looking it over again.

"I'm new in town, and I didn't have a chance to update it."

That seemed to catch Mrs. James's interest more than anything.

"Well, why didn't you say that? Between you and me, I believe that transplants like you understand the commitment we are looking for. Though it's temp, we need stable temps. I'd rather hire a transplant because I know you have a lot more on the line, trying to make a way for yourself in a new city and all."

Nina nodded. "Definitely. Wherever you send me, I'll do what I can to learn and do the job."

"Let's talk facts," Mrs. James said as she sipped from a cup of coffee that sat on her desk. "You don't have a college degree and very little experience. Your computer skills are nonexistent. I have jobs, but with your type of background I can only get you about ten dollars per hour. If you can up your skills, you can probably earn as high as eighteen dollars per hour in a couple of months. So you're aware there are no big bucks at this point."

"Yes, that's fine."

Mrs. James looked through a couple of marked postcards in her hands. "I have a law firm located on Park Avenue and Fifty-first. They have a receptionist who is going out on leave for a week or so. She will train you on the phones. She's a doll. She'll get you up and running on Microsoft Word. It's really simple, answering phones, greeting, smiling, being on time," she stressed.

Nina thought it sounded great. "When can I start?"

"How's tomorrow morning at 9 A.M.?"

Nina shook Mrs. James's hand as the woman led her out of the office and gave her a card with the company details. "Call me if anything changes. And, Nina, keep up that good attitude you have. Lots of people wouldn't even walk in here with your poor skills, but you beat me with that smile and drive. Good luck."

Nina thanked her and God as she waited for the elevator down.

Downstairs, Nina met Zohanna, who was already sipping on a tall caramel macchiato. Nina ordered one, too, and joined her.

"How did it go?" Zohanna asked as soon as Nina sat down.

"I start tomorrow."

"Girl, that is good!" Zohanna said, giving her a high five. "A law firm?"

"Yup," Nina said as she stirred her coffee drink.

"Me, too, which one?"

"Oh, God, I forgot to ask her the name. She gave me a card with the address and all that."

"Is it on Fifty-first and Park?" Zohanna asked, securing her lips around the cup.

"Yes, it is. Are you there?"

"Girl, yes for the third time! I like it," she said, giving Nina another high five. Nina laughed at Zohanna, who was obviously a happy camper after her sour complaints this morning. "At least I have someone to lunch with."

"Yeah," Nina said, curious to learn more about her. She had never met a female who was so friendly to another female. "Are you always like this?"

Zohanna bit into her coffee cake and wiped her mouth. "Yes, I mean, I cannot be shy when I can dance in a room of fifty men while shaking my ass up and down for a dollar. I worked with women all the time, so I know how to talk to a sister. Except, some of these bitches out here be so sour."

"You mean like you *were* this morning?"

Zohanna laughed. "At least I talked, right?"

"True."

Zohanna advised Nina about the protocol of Lawrence, Paige & Swaithe, the law firm they were both assigned to. Being a former temp there, she knew the ropes. Nina listened carefully about what to wear, how to act, and who not to talk to. Their conversation was light and carefree as they chatted for another ten minutes. But Nina wondered if their paths had crossed for a reason.

twenty-one

Lamont was working from home today, but with Ansley in his bed, he was unable to get much done. Every time he looked at Ansley, he wanted her to be Nina. The day they made love for the first time that Sunday at his home, he fell in love with her. He thought he may have loved her since the day he met her over fifteen years ago. He could care less what his mother said about Nina's rape, or even her connection to her ex-husband's death. After he had thought about it, he realized if he had been in her shoes, he probably would've kept that under wraps, too. He was scared of how much he felt for her, that at any moment he thought he was being played. But he was learning from Nina, while she thought she was learning from him.

He considered himself lucky to have met Nina at this point in his life, with a stable career, a new home, and a bright future. Nina was different from the other women he had been with—she was lively, sexual, and feminine. To him, she had an innocence about her that he hadn't seen in a woman. She was bright eyed and he admired that she was ambitious about starting a business of her own in the future. And he wanted to help her. She was good enough to be his girlfriend, but bad enough with a feisty edginess to keep him interested. Though he didn't tell her, he also didn't mind waiting for some of her sweet thing. He just didn't understand her, as he didn't understand most women. Ansley lay in his bed like she was the only woman in his life. He had explained to her that there was Nina, but it didn't seem to faze her from giving up some sex. But Ansley had a man, too, and played her position. She had popped up early this morning with bagels and no panties. But for him, sex with Ansley meant nothing. It helped him keep his emotions in check for Nina, who he thought had run away with his heart.

Lamont tapped away at his computer, but couldn't focus. He looked out his den window, but the streets on this early Saturday morning were still asleep. He was stark naked, and grabbed the closest thing to him, a bedroom sheet. He was worried that Nina might need him, since she had lost her job. He wondered if she had already found work. He dialed her number.

"Good morning," he said, taking a deep breath. "Asleep?"

"Well," she said with a yawn, "it *is* like 6 A.M."

He thought she'd be happier to hear from him. "Maybe I should send a text message."

"No, this is okay," Nina said, sounding more awake with every word. "Are you speaking to me now?"

"I always was. Do you need money?"

"I told you that I was fine. I made a way for myself," she said.

"Do you wanna tell me?" He looked over his shoulder at Ansley snoring like a three-hundred-pound man. He was known for putting women out for the count after laying it down in the bed. Except with Nina.

"I got a temp job."

"A temp job?" he said, feeling awful. He pictured Nina shuffling papers in a dirty mailroom.

"It's a receptionist job at a law firm. I had to do something for now," she said, yawing again.

"What firm?"

"Lawrence, Paige—"

Lamont cracked up laughing. "I have an appointment there Monday morning."

"I started a few days ago," Nina said, like she hadn't heard him.

He regained his cool. "Congrats, good luck. Call me if you need me."

He heard Nina's breath, like she wanted to say more. She wouldn't hang up.

He didn't say anything either. He wanted her to talk to him.

"I love you," she finally said, and the call disconnected.

Lamont sat there for five minutes as he absorbed Nina's words. Then a cool finger slid down his bald head. "I'm cold," Ansley purred, her long, brown, highlighted hair gathered in a high ponytail and her hips jutting out to a perfect shape. She bent over and led him back to the bed, where he couldn't get hard for her again. It didn't take long before Ansley got the message and bounced. It was then Lamont realized exactly the power Nina had over him. He was sure he wouldn't be hearing from Ansley anytime soon.

Later on that evening, about 8 P.M., Nina was polishing her toenails. She hoped she and Lamont would see each other this weekend. It annoyed her that he didn't come right over after they had hung up this morning. The last few days of work had been fine, but being surrounded by lawyers all day made it harder for her to stop thinking about him. His call this morning didn't mean things were back to normal. They had to sit down and have a talk about things. She was still betting that he'd call her to meet for lunch on Monday while he was at the office, but maybe he had other plans, she thought as she blew down her nails. But the ball was in her court, and she was ready to make the next move.

The bell rang. It was Lamont, she thought with a smile as she picked up some stray underwear in the bathroom. "I'll be right there!" she shouted when the bell rang again. "Coming!" Nina managed to get her empty apartment looking half decent in the forty-five seconds before she opened the door.

She flung it open and it was Zohanna. "Hey," Nina said in a long, drawn-out way. She had forgotten that Zohanna had driven her home from work Friday, and she didn't recall giving her an open invitation.

"Whatsup, girl!" Zohanna said, with a brown bag in her hand. "I was in the neighborhood seeing my auntie and I remembered you lived right up the block."

Nina held the door open telling herself she should've never opened it, but Zohanna was here, and she wasn't about to turn her away like a dog. "Come in."

"I hope you like Thai food, because I stopped at the takeout place on Flatbush," she said, sitting on a beanbag on the floor because Nina had no table and the couch was full of clothes.

Nina was definitely hungry, having survived most of the day on gummy bears. She hadn't seen Ms. Bauer today and missed the food. Nina grabbed a few foldout tables to spread the food on. Her eyes feasted on the shrimp pad thai, cartons of rice, steamed dumplings, and other goodies.

It wasn't Lamont like she wanted, but it was the food she needed. Zohanna pulled out some plates from the bag as they shared the dinner between them. They ate for a while without saying much, until Zohanna came up for air from the shrimp pad thai.

"So you ready for work Monday?" Zohanna asked, chewing with her mouth open. "I ain't. I swear all of those partners drive me up the wall. I'm only a temp, what do they want? My firstborn?"

Nina saw that the first few days had been hard for Zohanna because she was replacing a legal secretary and her job was more demanding, assisting two partners.

"Nobody bothers me besides the wives who have to get through right away to ask their husbands some dumb-ass question. I hope I'm never like that."

"That's why I love the desk. I just answered phones and read my magazines and flirted with the cute FedEx guys."

"You mean the big, fat Hispanic one?" Nina said, squeezing a packet of soy sauce on a steamed dumpling.

"Not him. There was another one, looked just like 50 Cent. You know, tall, dark, got that thug thing to 'em."

Nina was very familiar with that and figured that was what all New York women liked. "I like my men a little more old-fashioned-looking," Nina said, envisioning Lamont's distinguished, masculine look. "And I don't need my man getting into any trouble besides the trouble I'm giving him." Nina laughed as she began to enjoy Zohanna's company. After a few months, she thought it was about time to make a female friend. The only thing was that Zohanna didn't like talking about her past, but that was all right by Nina.

"You got a man?" Zohanna asked.

"Yeah, but we going through a little something right now. I'm also newly divorced."

Zohanna guzzled down her iced tea drink. "Damn, girl, you

waste no time. Divorced by twenty-five? I am thirty-four and I have never been married, never been asked, and never want to be asked, thank you," Zohanna said as she rolled her eyes.

"To each his own."

"Does he have his own place?" Zohanna asked.

"Yes, and it's much more comfortable than mine. He has furniture, for starters."

"Whowee, sounds like a keeper. Does he rent or own?"

"Own."

"Nice. Is he straight?"

"Yes!" Nina said, laughing uncomfortably.

Zohanna scooped a load of noodles up with her chopsticks. "Just playing, girl. I am taking a break from these men. How the hell did you get one so quick and you only been in New York three months?"

"We met at my job. I can't even explain it. I guess it was meant to be."

"He must be a real special brother. Dudes these days ain't even thinking about being in no relationship. Why you ain't both together tonight?"

"We had a little mishap, but we're working on it."

"And he ain't here? Oh, no, let me get my ass up," Zohanna said, like she was getting ready to leave. "You're too nice to tell me I am getting in the way of you getting some!"

"Not at all," Nina said, motioning for her to sit back down. "You are not stopping my man from coming by. We're fighting. But I think we're gonna make up soon. He has an appointment at the law firm."

"For what?" she said, half-interested.

"He's a lawyer." Nina was nonchalant about it. She didn't want to make it seem like it was a big deal to her.

"A lawyer? Is he black?"

"Yes!" Nina said, looking at Zohanna like she was out of her mind.

"A single black lawyer in New York City who can commit? I can't wait till Monday. That I gotta see."

twenty-two

Ahmasi had a special box in his apartment dedicated to Nina. In it were several strands of Nina's pubic hair he'd collected from his pillows and sheets, a loose gold button, some bobbie pins, and a soiled panty. These were things he gathered without her knowing during her stays with him. The soiled panty he stole out of her purse one night, on a sleepover. He brought the panty to his nose and inhaled the scent that he had protected in a plastic Ziploc. It smelled like salty bleach and he tasted it on his tongue. He savored Nina when she was with him, and when she was without him. He carefully assembled the items back in the black box and checked the time. It was 3 A.M. It was exactly the same hour when he had killed Trent. The evening came back all too suddenly for him, as the thought of what went down keyed him up.

He and Trent had gotten into a bad fight about Nina. Trent refused to give him the money because he had been seeing her. After Ahmasi beat him to a pulp in the alley of the pool hall, he stuffed his unconscious body down in his trunk, bashed his head in with some bricks, and drowned his body in the darkness of the creek. He changed his clothes, dumped the car, and walked eight miles to the nearest gas station where he hitched a ride to the airport. He did that all in less than three hours. A woman named Rebecca had sent him the money a few days before by Western Union but Ahmasi never told Trent that. He was a pro at this. It wasn't the first time he had killed.

He didn't want to be this way, but in his head people made him do the darndest things. His poetry had always been an outlet, but also his mask. He believed it was what got Nina to open up and let down her guard for him. The romantic, sensitive, charming poet game was one he had down pat. The Teacup Lounge was where he met most of his women, and where he took them for a little R & R. Nina was special. She could see that there was more to him than met her eye. He didn't expect her to dump him as fast as she did, but the cards were already dealt. He couldn't stand that Trent was her husband. He beat him down for money, but killed him for her.

The money he left Nina was his peace offering. He thought she could've at least called and thanked him. He lit another blunt and pictured her face, how she must've looked when she saw the check. *Bitch.* She'd been high and mighty, he thought, at the coffee shop when she told him to leave her alone, but all about the Benjamins when the time came. *Just like everybody else.* He pictured her spending the money on the new man in her life and blew out a circle of smoke for each letter of her name. *Whore.* He was in love with her without a doubt. It wasn't a love that anyone else could understand. He could smell her when she was afar and see inside her soul when she was near. *Bitch, bitch, bitch.* As he fought back the rage he felt, tears flowed down his eyes. He wanted her badly. Rejection was something he had always gotten from women, and that was that, but men had always been easier. There were only a few male lovers in his past, but that was then. He wanted to start a new life with Nina. *My angel.* But he knew it was a fantasy. She would never want him, but, he thought, maybe if she only knew how he really felt, things could change.

He called her.

"Hello?" he said when she answered.

"Who is this?" she asked, alarmed.

"It's Ahmasi," he whispered as he unbuckled his pants. "Can I talk to you?"

Nina sighed. "What do you want?"

"How's the money, honey?" He smiled, cradling his massive dick in his hand. The sound of her voice aroused him rock solid.

This time Nina didn't say anything.

"Please talk to me." His voice was low as he stroked the length of his dick.

"I got the money, thank you," she mumbled.

Ahmasi spread his legs out as he pumped his dick until moisture seeped from the opening. He panted heavily. "Nina, I need you right now."

"You are crazy," she said.

"My dick is so hard right now I could bust through this phone into your mouth."

Next thing he heard was the dial tone. He called back.

She didn't answer, but he got her voice mail. He jacked off hard, his right hand around his dick like a vise grip to a voice on the recording that was soothing and sweet. After the beep he said, "I need you, Nina, I can see you right here sitting on my dick," he said, a release rising inside him. A tear fell from his eye. "Why you acting like this? I only been good to you. But you fucked me over. You used me." He massaged his dick harder, with quick, flicking strokes.

"But I'll show you what it means to fuck with the wrong man," he said, and gasped. "Oh, shit, whoooo!" he said into the phone as it fell out of his hand. A line of white, creamy fluid streamed down his dick. It was the best sex he had had with Nina in a while.

The following morning, Nina found herself at the police precinct before work. She tried to file an order of protection, but it was impossible. They couldn't do it unless there was a prior history of assault.

"I can't believe this," she cried on the phone to Dee, who she called immediately. Dee knew all the background stuff. Nina didn't have the time to tell anyone else the story from the beginning.

"You know I would be the first one to tell you to do what you gotta do," Dee said. "And I still believe that fool is crazy, but he really didn't do anything the cops could help with."

Nina crossed the street at Atlantic Avenue to the train station. It was raining and there was no way she wanted to be late this morning. Being late was the last thing she needed. "You should've heard him panting and breathing on my phone like he was jacking off on my machine. He said something about showing me he ain't the one to fuck with. What does all that mean?"

"It probably mean his ass was drunk. People do drunk dialing all the time," Dee reassured her. "He knows where you live. I would've thought by now he would've done something. I think the next time he calls curse his ass out like a sailor! If you got to put your new man on the phone, whatever!"

Nina thought about it and it might not be a bad idea, but she had an eerie feeling about it all. "Dee, he sounded like he was fucking me and crying. It's like he had a breakdown." Nina followed the crowd across another street to the train entrance.

"Tell him he has a small dick, that will shut him down," Dee said, angry as hell.

Nina's umbrella flew away. "Oh, shit," she said, watching it cascade down the block in the wind. "That's not gonna work, not with a man who knows he's holding a monster. Let me go, girl. I'll keep you posted."

"Just call me and I'll be down there with a .38," Dee said with light humor. "Take it easy. Just stay away from him and change your numbers if you have to."

Nina ended the call as she finally reached the train station. The number four was there as if it was waiting all along for her to arrive. She slipped in between the closing doors.

When Nina arrived at work, she was five minutes early. She quickly gathered herself together, put the newspapers out, and updated the office attendance list that noted who was out sick, on vacation, or away at a client's. Before she sat down behind the desk and secured her earpiece, she checked her voice mail. She had thirty-seven missed calls in an hour, and two messages that were both hang ups. It was Ahmasi. His call was identified each time. Once her boards lit up, Nina tucked her phone away. Her mind was spinning. She was even afraid to pick up the office phones.

It crossed her mind to call Lamont. She had to tell him what was going down. Maybe he could help her sort it out. When she reached for the phone to dial him, she remembered he was coming to the office today. She checked the visitor list, and she saw that the office manager had put his name down, but no time. Nina inputted the information into the security database.

"Good morning, Ms. Thang," Zohanna said as she stopped by Nina's desk on her way to make one of the partners coffee.

"Good morning for you maybe," Nina said during a quiet time between the phones. "But I barely made it in here this morning. I had the most ridiculous night. I couldn't sleep."

"The boyfriend again?" Zohanna asked, tapping her black, manicured nails on the desk. "Speaking of, isn't he coming today?"

"Yes, he is, but this ain't about him. You ever have someone who can't leave you alone?" Nina did know that she was revealing it at the least opportune place, at work, but she had so much boiled up inside her, it was spilling over. She needed to talk to someone.

Zohanna leaned in over the desk. "And you got a stalker now? Girl, you gotta tell me your secret," she said with a smile.

"I'm serious, Zohanna. This guy jacked off on the phone on my voice mail threatening me and telling me he wants me."

"What's the problem?" Zohanna had a blank look.

Nina looked at her absent eyes. "Nothing, forget it."

Zohanna leaned in deeper. "Does your man know? Just have him pick up the phone next time."

"Lamont is not that kind of guy and I don't want this to get ugly," Nina said as she picked up a call.

After she transferred, she said to Zohanna, "I'm scared. He called me thirty-seven times already."

Zohanna waved her hand. "Sounds to me like he did some drunken dialing and then thought about how stupid he sounded, and is calling you now to apologize. Let it go. He seems like a weirdo. A man who's gonna really hurt you ain't gonna *warn* you."

Several lines lit up at once. Nina managed all of them, clicking a button as the next one was put on hold. Zohanna took her cue and commenced to finish her morning duties, too. For a while, everything was back to normal.

twenty-three

It was 4:30 p.m. and Nina hadn't seen Lamont. She didn't miss him because she had asked Zohanna to cover for her while she was at lunch. Nina checked the visitor list and didn't see his name. Nina called him, but got no answer. She was getting off in thirty minutes.

As the phones died down, she looked at the clock and realized maybe he had changed his appointment around to avoid her. But just then, the glass doors to the reception area flew open.

"Out of all the law firms in the world," Lamont said, gliding in at 4:45. His eyes brightened when he smiled at her.

But Nina didn't smile, she started crying. "I'm so sorry," she said.

"No, I'm sorry." He reached over and grabbed her hand. He gave her the clean handkerchief that he carried only as an accessory. "But this is not the place."

Nina nodded and composed herself. "Who are you here to see?" she asked him, like she did all visitors.

He backed off the receptionist desk when two young male associates walked by. "I'm here to see Mr. Waithe."

"Okay, one moment," Nina said, in her professional manner. "Have a seat, please."

She pressed the numbers to Mr. Waithe's secretary and Zohanna picked up. "I have Mr. Franklin in the reception area to see Mr. Waithe."

Zohanna told her she'd be right out.

Lamont approached her desk again. "Can we get together after this? I'll only be about a half hour."

"Of course," Nina said, wanting to feel his chest against her face again. "We need to talk about *a lot* of things—"

"Mr. Franklin?" Zohanna said as she appeared. "I'm Mr. Waithe's temporary assistant, Zohanna." Then Zohanna looked at Nina who had a big grin. "You're Nina's man!" she said, pointing at him.

Lamont was noticeably embarrassed as he looked down at his shoes with a little smile. "Hi, Zohanna, nice to meet you."

"Oh, no, call me Zoe," she said, squeezing his hand, and she walked with him without letting go of it.

Lamont waved to Nina with a look asking her where Zohanna came from. Nina wasn't quite sure, either. Zohanna finally let go of his hand and escorted Nina's man to the conference room with a strut that she was seeing for the first time.

Nina and Lamont had one of the best curried lamb dinners at a chic South African restaurant in Harlem that was an "in" place after the *New York Times* gave it rave reviews weeks ago. But Lamont insisted he had been going there before the masses who now waited weeks for a table.

"Do you hate me?" was the first thing Lamont asked when they finally sat down across from each other.

"I hate this mess that I caused, but I don't hate you. I want to be with you and only you," Nina said.

"What does that mean exactly?" Lamont asked, unfolding his African printed table napkin.

"It means that I realize what's important to me. I don't know what tomorrow holds," she said, with a flashing thought of Ahmasi. "How I've been acting, not being open with you, hasn't been fair—"

"Me, too, I've been demanding way too much," he said.

Her shoulders dropped. "Do you still love me?"

"Yes." He sipped his glass of red wine and flashed a brilliant smile.

Nina sliced into a piece of her lamb dish. She had almost forgotten how exceptionally handsome he was, with his perfectly groomed goatee and suckable lips. Though his answer was only one word, in his eyes was so much more.

"You look good today. Did you dress for me?" he teased. "You know I like the color red on a woman."

"Oh, I just threw this on," she said, referring to her cranberry red and white-trimmed, sleeveless summer dress.

Then his demeanor became serious. "I need to tell you something."

"Me first," Nina said as she put her fork down.

"No, please," he insisted. He wiped some moisture from the food off his lips with the napkin. "I had sex with someone else while we were apart."

Nina's mouth flew open, but the words didn't come out. And she was glad they didn't. "Who was it?"

"It doesn't matter. I just want you to know that will never happen again—"

Nina signaled him to stop speaking. She didn't want him making promises that would come back to haunt the both of them. She had to let it go. "I see, but I guess we were broken up, so—" she said, her voice trailing off. If she didn't have dirt of her own, she would've probably dug her fork into his hand. But she didn't want to scold him for being honest, either.

"Is there anything else?" she asked, grinding her tension-filled jaw.

He shook his head. "But by your reaction, I guess you're gonna tell me there was someone else, too?"

"Not exactly," Nina corrected him. "But I will tell you that I saw Ahmasi again. That guy who supposedly killed my ex-husband."

Lamont's forehead wrinkled like paper. "What for? Why would you even have a conversation with him?"

Nina explained about the day she was at Michelle's, when she bumped into Ahmasi. She also told him about the money.

"You gotta pay him back. We can mail it to him tomorrow, FedEx, overnight, whatever," Lamont said, speaking quickly. "I don't want that man to have anything over you. Why didn't you ask me?" he said, infuriated.

"I didn't plan to ask anyone. He left the money. And to be honest, I deserved half of what Trent had, and I let it go. I deserved to keep a few measly thousand."

Lamont moved his head up and down. "So it's like a divorce settlement?" he asked in an almost mimicking fashion.

"If you wanna call it that, you can. But the point is I never asked for it."

"Fine, keep it," Lamont said, seemingly giving up. "But anytime he comes back to you, let me know. I can give that brother a check in no time."

"But there's more." Nina revealed about the harassing phone calls.

Lamont was far more concerned about this than anything else. "Did you call the police?"

Finally, she thought, there was someone who was seeing it her way. "I will, the next time it happens, but I'm changing my numbers."

"Good, and I have an idea," he said, stroking her face. "Why don't you move in with me?"

"Because of Ahmasi?"

"Maybe, but I think if you could save some money, I can match it two or three times, and we can open up that salon you always wanted."

Nina's knees knocked the table as she jumped out of her seat to hug him. "Are you serious, baby?" She couldn't think of a better way to get back together with him.

"I have a list of clients, friends, so we don't have to worry about getting clients."

"Thank you," Nina said as she sat on his lap and secured kisses all over his face. Several people in the restaurant stared at them, and whispered. But at this point, there was nothing on her mind but getting back home.

On the drive back in Lamont's BMW that he rarely ever drove, Nina noticed the front page of the New York *Daily News.* It read, "Family Massacred in Love Triangle." Nina flipped through the pages after she read her horoscope. As he turned the corner on Chambers to hop on the Brooklyn Bridge, she felt faint reading the story.

"What's wrong?" Lamont asked when he saw Nina's face turn pale. The sun was setting over the river as Nina looked down at the water. She had lost somebody else to death.

"The girl I used to work with, Melanie, and her family, were murdered," Nina said, going back to the article as Lamont sat in rush-hour traffic over the bridge. "Her whole family was murdered by her lover Javier. She told me how kind and nice he was."

Lamont snatched the paper and read halfway down the article before the car moved again. "Sorry about this, Nina. Are you gonna find out about the funeral?"

"Definitely," Nina said in a daze. "When I got fired, I gave her my number in a note, but I didn't hear anything. Now I know why," Nina said, shaking her head. Javier was supposed to be the man who Melanie trusted, the man who didn't beat her, but loved her. It was the people you least expected, Nina thought, who have the most surprises.

Melanie's funeral was held a week later in Bay Ridge, Brooklyn, inside a small chapel with stained glass windows. Lamont accompanied her. The church was dark, and the dark wood and paintings made it seem cold and unfeeling. Nina expected lots of folks, maybe even some of the people from the job. But no one came, not even Delores. Just Melanie's kids, her parents, family members, and some strangers who read about it in the papers. Nina sat with Lamont all the way in the back. She cried and smiled a little as she listened to the Hispanic priest carry on about sin and redemption. His loud, booming voice was condemning. It was as if everyone accepted that Melanie had asked for this. That she had made her own bed and had to sleep in it, or, rather, die in it. The priest ended with a supplication that God forgive Melanie for her sins in time to enter heaven's gate; there was nothing said of the brutality that she'd endured. Nina waited for family members to stand up for Melanie, at least to share a good story about the woman. But no one had stories. Everyone just sulked and listened to the heavy-handed priest. Before the service ended, Nina stood up.

"I have something to say about Melanie," Nina said as she approached the altar. Nina could hear the whispers and feel the glare from the eyes that followed her down the dark walkway. She knew they weren't looking at her clothes, because she wore a traditional black dress that was long and modest. It was actually one Lamont had bought her the other day.

Nina cleared her throat and stepped up to the microphone. She didn't look into anyone's eyes, not even Lamont's, but straight ahead. "I'm Nina, one of Melanie's friends from work," she began. She shared Melanie's qualities as a person: a good listener, a nurturer, and a friend. After three minutes, she had made her peace. Lamont stood up as she took her seat beside him. Once the priest was done with his blessings, Nina and Lamont paid their respects to Melanie's family. They didn't speak English, but their smiles told her that they were pleased. And so was Nina.

twenty-four

Nina spent the rest of the week sulking in her apartment. Melanie's death took a toll on her and made her more paranoid about Ahmasi, who she thankfully hadn't heard back from. She had changed her cell phone number yesterday and made sure Dee had it so she could pass it on to her mother for emergencies only.

"Nina, you in here?" she heard Ms. Bauer call through her door. Nina climbed out of bed and looked through the peephole.

"Hi, Ms. Bauer. Where you been?" Nina said, holding her door open, and Ms. Bauer walked in.

"Nice," Ms. Bauer said, her fat brown arms folded against her chest and her familiar furry house slippers on. "You keeping this place good."

"Thank you." Nina realized that this was Ms. Bauer's first time in her place, to her knowledge, at least. "What can I do for you?"

"No, baby," Ms. Bauer said, holding her beige house robe

around her. "I came to see if there was anything you needed. I was away at my young niece's graduation from college. She graduated from Spellman."

"Oh, that's nice, Ms. Bauer, but I'm okay. I take it you spoke to Dee."

"Yes, I did, and she said that dreads boy been giving you problems. If he ever comes here, I'm calling the cops." Ms. Bauer's nose wrinkled up into a tight knot on her face.

"That makes two, but everything seems fine. I don't want you to worry about me," Nina said, feeling bad that she could be causing the old woman stress. This was not what she wanted. "Actually, Ms. Bauer, I wanted to tell you that I plan on moving."

Ms. Bauer's smile quickly turned down. "What for?" She couldn't possibly see what reason Nina could give. "Is it the dread boy?"

"No, it's my boyfriend. We decided to live together so I can save," Nina said, feeling good about making the move.

"He proposed yet?"

Nina took a step back. Ms. Bauer was good at catching her off guard with her boldness. But a proposal wasn't exactly what Nina was holding out for. "We haven't discussed that."

"You don't want to get married again, I guess," Ms. Bauer said.

But it was too late for Nina. She had a plan that not even Lamont could get in the way of. "I just need to do this now, Ms. Bauer. I gotta get my finances in check and get stable again. I can't survive on a temp job. I didn't come to New York for that."

Ms. Bauer sat herself down on Nina's yellow futon. "Did you come here to shack up?"

Nina sat next to her. "I came here to build a future for myself that was different than anyone else's in my family and in my small town. Lamont, my boyfriend, is a good man who loves me. I can stay with him until I get things straight."

"Is that what this young man wants, too?"

"He wants to help me so we can possibly build a future together. With or without him, I know I will be okay, because I'll always have my own."

"Like a savings account?"

"Exactly, and I'm building on that," Nina said as she recounted the five thousand dollars she had deposited weeks ago.

"Just don't end up pregnant," Ms. Bauer said as she got up to leave. "But from what it sounds like, you may have a man who loves you."

"Yeah, I'm feeling pretty good about this," Nina said, holding the door open for her. "I'll give you another month's rent for the short notice."

"Child, please. It was a pleasure having you but I won't be renting out to no more folks," she said, waving her finger around. "I am here if you need me."

"Thanks, Ms. Bauer."

That afternoon Lamont was taking Nina on a luxury world-class yacht, where a couple of his firm's new clients were meeting. Nina put on her best face, though Melanie's death was still very much a part of her. Lamont suggested that her coming with him might lift her spirits and maybe he was right. She wore a white flowing skirt and sleeveless camisole that accentuated her breasts and hips. She wanted to make the best impression on Lamont's associates, and on Lamont, too.

The *Santa Maria,* the yacht which Lamont's associate owned, was standing by waiting when Nina and Lamont arrived at the pier. It was just before dark on Sunday at around 7:30. The evening was balmy, and a thin veil of darkness was slowly descending on the city.

"Come on over!" cheered Louie as he waved from the deck of the yacht.

"He's mighty cheerful," Nina said as she held on to the bend of Lamont's arm.

"He's probably had a few drinks already. This guy is loaded. What else can he do with his time on that boat?"

"What would you do?" Nina asked.

"Sleep." He laughed as they hurried their pace to climb the steps to the yacht.

Louie stood at the top, looking casual in a blue shirt and plaid pants. He flicked the ashes from his cigar as he waved some more at them. He wiped his hands on his sides as they finally walked up to him. "If you don't mind, Lamont, I'd rather shake this beautiful lady's hand first," Louie said.

"This is my girlfriend, Nina Bettus." Lamont let Nina step forward as she put her hand out for Louie to shake, but he kissed it.

"Welcome, beautiful," Louie said, setting a wet, cold one on her.

"Thank you," Nina said as she faked a smile.

"Louie is a partner at Cromwell & Sutton," Lamont told her, and Nina quickly checked herself. She recalled that Lamont worked for one of the top law firms in the country.

"So nice to meet you," Nina said, smiling more warmly. "I can't wait to see the rest of this beautiful yacht."

"Come, come, I can't wait to show the both of you," he said, putting his arm through Nina's. "I want you both to meet some people. Especially you, Lamont." Louie escorted them upstairs to the top deck. "Wait here. Enjoy the view until I get the other guests."

Nina sat down on a bench. "Is he a partner, for real?"

"Yeah, I know, he's a little eccentric. He's real nice on the outside, but he's a genius of the law. There's nothing he can't make happen. He has nearly every CEO on the Forbes 100 eating out of his hand," Lamont said as they both looked over the waters lapping up against the sides of the yacht. The sea was a bluish black as the night fell upon them. "But I'm gonna get his job one day."

Lamont's stern look startled Nina, like he was plotting Louie's demise.

"One day," Lamont said again as he caught Nina's quizzical look at him. "When he least expects it."

"I thought you liked Louie," Nina said, taking Lamont's words as healthy competition between friends.

"I learned a lot from that man. Let's just leave it at that," Lamont said as a huge wave crashed against the boat, making them jump back to avoid getting wet. Lamont wrapped his arm around Nina as they kept their attention on the water. The tide had picked up and so had the winds.

Louie walked onto the deck with another man and woman. "There's too much wind up here," Louie said, holding his toupee.

Lamont and Nina tried to hold in their laughter, but couldn't, so they coughed to hide it.

"Let's go to the bar," Louie said, putting his age-spotted hands on the woman's naked, bony knees. "This is my girlfriend, Ansley Jones, and Frank Weiser, VP of Milton & Hanson, the number one banking corporation in the country."

"Oh, hello," Nina said, shaking everyone's hand as they greeted her and Lamont. She tried her best to conceal the shock of Louie's girlfriend being a black woman, and a young one like her, at that. The woman must have been at least twenty-five years his junior.

But she realized that Ansley's gaze never fell too far from

Lamont, and when they shook hands, she could sense that it wasn't a first meeting. Then it all hit her right there. *Ansley. Ansley?* It was the name she had heard on his voice mail months ago. Nina lost her footing and nearly tripped as the boat rocked. But that wasn't the only thing she lost at that moment.

Everyone followed Louie down the steps as Nina checked out Ansley from behind. She was decked out in what looked like a designer linen dress trimmed in gold with matching gold bangles and necklace. She was tall, about five-foot nine, slender, with a bushel of thick, long, healthy brown hair with light streaks in it. Nina didn't feel like she could match up to this woman who was in a whole different league. If she had known Ansley looked like this she would've started a bigger fuss about her months ago. It was Lamont's arm around Nina the entire time that provided her with the security she thought she needed.

They all ordered drinks, and in moments the pitch in the room raised. Nina had two shots of tequila and soon she looked like just another chick from the block. They made some polite exchange, but for some reason Ansley wouldn't stand too close to her. Lamont was busy talking to Frank and Louie, which forced Ansley and Nina to find their common ground. The men excused themselves to the parlor room to smoke cigars and strategize to get Mr. Weiser's account and discuss his needs. This left Nina with no choice.

Ansley sat with her legs crossed on the other side of the boat, sipping a glass of champagne as she avoided her. Nina walked over to her side and sat opposite, staring her in the face.

Ansley continued ignoring her.

"I'm just gonna get right to the point," Nina said, taking a sip out of her shot glass of tequila. "Did you or did you not?"

"Did I what?" Ansley said with a phony smile. Her eyelashes were so long and thick they looked like wings when she batted them.

"Did you fuck Lamont?" Nina was lubricated enough to not feel a tinge of embarrassment about her question.

Ansley couldn't compete with Nina's holding stare, and looked away again.

"Don't make me ask you again." She could tell that Ansley wasn't the fighting type, but a calculating one. But Nina had no time for mind games; one more tequila and she would be in fighting mode.

Ansley sighed and said at last, "We did, but—"

Nina expected her to be defiant, but Ansley was soft-spoken, almost in a sad way. "But what?"

"Lamont loves you, Nina, and what happened between us was a fluke."

"What do you mean?"

"Look, I answered your question," Ansley said, poised and tight-lipped. "I don't need to tell you my life story. I was with Lamont before Louie and I got back together."

"When was the last time you were with Lamont?"

"A few months ago when he was broken up with you—"

"We weren't officially broken up," Nina pointed out. "And he already told me."

"So why did you ask?"

"I wanted to be sure."

"Sure of what?" Ansley said, losing some of her cool. "Lamont loves you. He couldn't get his dick hard for me on our second round. I guess he had just gotten off the phone with you."

Nina didn't know how to respond to that. Damn, she told herself, Lamont was good. Lamont told her the honest truth, knowing that perhaps this day would come. She had nothing new she could go back to catch him on. There was nothing she could say to him because he wasn't caught. This had never happened to her before. "I see," was all Nina could think of.

"He told you already, right?" Ansley guessed.

"Yeah, and we worked it out. I just didn't expect to see you. Ever."

"Well, get used to it," Ansley said as she showed off her fat diamond engagement ring. It looked like it was at least nine carats. "Louie and I just got engaged."

"Does he know about Lamont?"

"It's like an old boys club, nobody's sweating who's with you."

Nina didn't know whether to say congratulations or wish that she choked on her champagne. She was glad that Ansley was engaged and, from her tone, whatever she'd had with Lamont was indeed over. "Nice ring," Nina said, sounding unimpressed.

"Woman to woman, Nina. I don't know you, nor do I have to know you to tell you this," Ansley said as the rest of the champagne disappeared into her mouth. She set the glass down. "You are dealing with a power broker. That's what all of these men on this boat are, and the men that they deal with, too. It may look all fine and dandy, but don't start snooping around asking the wrong questions. They will tell you what you need to know, and what you don't need to know, you shouldn't ask."

"What does that mean?" Nina said, feeling privy to some code Ansley was letting her in on.

"It means play your position. Men like Lamont will never be 'caught out there.' These are high-powered TV-land lawyers who cover their tracks and set their sights on what they want and get it. Being a woman in their life means giving up your own."

Nina didn't know if what Ansley was saying was good. She didn't want to give up her own life for anyone. "I think that is up to the individual woman and I choose to have my own line of work. I don't want to be dependent on anyone."

"It's not a bad thing, Nina," Ansley said as she took out a mirror from her purse to adjust her hair. "Lamont is a good catch. He's one of the few men who will actually let you do what you want to do. Just give him what he wants."

"How do you know him like this?"

"I don't, I just know his kind."

twenty-five

Nina was on week three of her temp assignment. Every day she and Zohanna had lunch, and every day Zohanna asked her about Lamont. Nina didn't mind talking about him, but she kept his bed skills to herself. After that incident with Ansley, she just wasn't sure who anybody was anymore, except Lamont. She didn't bring up the Ansley incident, but they both knew silently that a conversation did take place. But she thanked him inside for telling her, and not making her look like a fool in front of another woman. Whatever Lamont's technique was, she was feeling it. As long as he didn't have any more "confessions" up his sleeve, neither would she.

A month after he asked, Nina moved the last of her things into his place. He had set everything up for her. She had her own room, where she'd exercise, read, or just hang out on the computer and sharpen her skills. They, of course, shared his bedroom, and everything else in his home she had reign over, including his phone and mail. They even shopped for her favorite foods, and he cooked at night when he felt like it or she'd meet him in the city for dinner if he was working late, which was the story since he and Louie secured the Milton & Hanson account. Lamont was the major force behind the acquisition and it raised his profile to another level. And he planned to surprise Nina with a very personal gift.

Dee was in town this weekend. Her timing was a bit off because Nina had only been living with Lamont for a few days when she called from the Marriott in Times Square. She was only here for a few hours on a stopover because she was going to D.C. for a conference for African-American businesswomen. They decided to meet up in the city for brunch. Nina invited Zohanna, too.

All three ladies sat outside a quaint, Italian sidewalk café in Tribeca as they sipped mimosas and feasted on savory meat and vegetable Italian dishes. It was a beautiful Saturday afternoon in June with the temperature reaching over eighty degrees. Nina was more than comfortable in simple blue wide-legged linen pants and matching sleeveless halter with a brand-new necklace with a diamond-encrusted pendant in gold and platinum that Lamont had bought.

The sidewalk was teeming with shoppers, pets, babies in carriages, and honking cars, but none of that could stop the flow of the conversations about everything from the latest fashions to celebrity gossip to Nina's man.

"So, girl, what is Lamont doing on this Saturday afternoon?" Dee asked as she bit down on her crunchy but chewy tomato and basil bruschetta.

"On Saturdays, he spends at least half the day in the gym, swimming, running, playing basketball. When I left him, he was going out for his morning jog," Nina said, something she wanted to start doing with him, too, especially with the few pounds she'd been gaining with all of their dining out.

Zohanna chimed in, "He sounds like Mr. Perfect." She picked out some crumbs that had fallen into the cleavage of her stretch white dress and put them in her mouth. "Tell her what he did today."

"He said the brunch was on him today. He's paying for it," Nina said, taking out her AmEx authorized user card. She hated showing off like this, but they made it too easy for her.

"My goodness, well, why didn't you tell me," Dee joked as she called for the young, slick-haired waiter who came quickly. "Can I have the shrimp seviche, the lobster box, and the shrimp and beef salad?"

"Right away," said the young man as he dashed off.

"As you were saying," Dee turned back to the conversation as they laughed.

Nina didn't have a problem treating them. It wasn't like every day she went out for brunch or went out with friends, period. She enjoyed how it made her feel.

"Shhh," she said to them as she noticed Lamont calling on her cell phone. "Hi, baby."

"Put him on speaker," Zohanna squealed.

"Baby, hold on," Nina said as she did just that. "Can you hear me?"

Lamont laughed as Dee and Zohanna both said at the same time, "Hii, Laaamont!"

"Whatsup, ladies, did somebody forget to invite me?" he asked playfully.

"No, but Dee just ordered three hundred dollars' worth of food."

"Just bring home the doggy bag," he said with a laugh. "Enjoy yourself, babe."

"I will!" she said, and hung up.

"He is so sweet!" Zohanna said again. "And he didn't even sweat the three hundred dollars."

" 'Cause he knew she was lying," Dee said, a little annoyed by Zohanna.

"Dee just ordered like thirty dollars," Nina said as the waiter laid down another round of mimosas.

"How is he about you going out?" Dee asked.

"He's fine. Zohanna and I went to an after-work comedy show and he didn't mind one bit when I got in after midnight. He just likes it when I call, that's all."

Dee grinned as her array of food was laid before her. "Mmm, this is lovely," Dee said, spooning up the seviche. "Y'all come have some of the lobster box and salad." But Nina was satisfied with her own crispy prawns entree that she had already started.

"But we have to see his mother again next week. The woman hates me because my father broke her heart," Nina said, getting flashbacks of that horrible day at her home.

Dee said, sucking a shrimp out of its shell, "Well, one thing I know, if Mama ain't happy, nobody's happy."

Nina had showered and dressed in her Sunday best on a Wednesday night. She was in a simple, soft lavender suit and white pearls. Lamont picked her up after work to drive to his mother's house. This was not a dinner that was planned. Nina was relieved, because she still wasn't excited about eating Mrs. Franklin's food. She made sure she had a healthy slice of pizza before she left with Lamont. She wanted the afternoon to go by quickly. Lamont promised her they wouldn't stay more than an hour.

Mrs. Franklin was gardening in her lush backyard when they arrived.

"Mommy, we're here," Lamont called out to her from the front.

Mrs. Franklin appeared immediately at the front door and let them in.

"Make yourselves comfortable. I just have to take off these gloves," she said, closing the door. "Didn't think you'd get here so fast."

Lamont and Nina sat down as Mrs. Franklin washed her hands and gloves in the kitchen. Nina looked around her home, impressed with her style and flair. Long palm leaves stuck out of vases adorned with colorful daisies and orchids. Her home was like an indoor garden full of sweet floral scents and a rainbow of colors. She wondered how a home so peaceful could harbor a woman so tormented.

"Do you want anything to drink?" she asked them, all the while looking at Lamont. She still had not given Nina any eye contact.

"We're fine. Actually, we want to talk to you."

"Oh," Mrs. Franklin said as she sat down on her soft chenille floral-printed couch. "What is it?"

"Hello, Mrs. Franklin. How are you?" Nina said, tired of being ignored.

"Sorry, darling. I should have said something to you earlier. Just a little flustered having worked in the backyard all day. It's not like I have a man around here to help."

"Well, Mommy. You know if you need help, you can call me."

"I know, and you're good at these things. I just don't want to be a bother." Mrs. Franklin gave Nina a plastered, fake smile as she studied her face. "How are you, dear?"

"Good, doing good," Nina said.

"Look, I want to apologize to you for my outburst last time. I have high blood pressure, and sometimes I can't stop myself. I was out of line," she said, talking to Lamont.

"It's not me you should be talking to," Lamont said.

Mrs. Franklin turned to Nina. "Sorry," she said.

Nina could tell he wanted this to be over as much as she did. They followed Mrs. Franklin to the dining room where she had a beautiful table set with Cornish hens, roasted potatoes, garden vegetables, and salad.

They all sat around the table as Mrs. Franklin said a quick grace over the food. Everyone wanted the evening to move along. Small talk about her garden and plans to travel this summer to Italy was light and easy.

Until Lamont revealed, "Nina and I live together now."

Mrs. Franklin's smile quickly faded. She was almost as pink in the face as her blouse. "What for?"

"For love." Lamont nodded at her. "People still do that these days. We may even get married."

Nina wondered if Lamont was trying to kill her. She tapped his foot under the table.

"Mrs. Franklin, I'm in between jobs right now and Lamont thought we could get together, save, and plan for our future," Nina said. "I hope we have your blessings." Nina was trying to keep the peace. She was actually enjoying the food, and didn't want to leave early again.

"Why do you need my blessings?" Mrs. Franklin snapped as she went back to her food.

"Nina is a woman with dignity. Any woman like that would want to come into a family the right way," Lamont said, holding Nina's hand.

"Well—" Mrs. Franklin stuck out her chin "—a woman with dignity wouldn't be moving in with you before marriage."

Lamont opened his mouth in Nina's defense, but Nina stepped up. "Mrs. Franklin, you don't know anything about me. Nor do you even try to. Did you know that Lamont asked me to move in with him? As soon as I did, he made me feel at home. All I want to do is love your son."

Mrs. Franklin's eyes scanned Nina's face for any sign of weakness. But Nina didn't even bat an eye.

"I have a problem with that because no one took the time to tell me. Sometimes I feel I'm not even a part of your life, Lamont," Mrs. Franklin said, her lips wrinkled in distaste.

"How can you be, when everything's a problem?" Lamont said. "Nothing or no one is ever good enough."

Nina sensed that this conversation had very little to do with her; this sounded like a mother-son thing that had been brewing for a while. She listened.

"Lamont, dear, all I am saying is I don't want to see you hurt. Please think this through," Mrs. Franklin practically begged him.

Nina's posture was getting weaker and weaker. *Was I that bad?* Nina fought to defend herself. "Mrs. Franklin, I understand where you are coming from as a mother who wants to see the best for her son—"

"Lamont has been married once already, and I don't want to see—"

"I understand, Mrs. Franklin. He and I both know better how to make a marriage work than we have in the past, and neither of us have intentions to hurt anyone. Not even you. When we're ready for marriage you'll be the first to know." This time she felt Lamont tap her foot.

Mrs. Franklin shook her head like she was in a bad dream. "I know it seems like I have some vendetta, Nina, I just don't really know you and—"

"Then get to know me. I want to get to know you, too," Nina said, seeing a possibility.

"I just think that I would want my son to do better. He used to date college-educated women, women who have degrees, do you know that?"

Before Nina could answer, Lamont said, "And the last woman like that I divorced. So what's your point?"

An unusual, serene look took over Mrs. Franklin's face. "You'll see for yourself. Right, Nina?"

"I don't know what you're talking about," she said, her appetite dead as a nail.

"Have you ever been with a man like Lamont? Do you know what he needs?" she asked. "His career is very stressful—"

This time Lamont stayed quiet.

"Lamont is a big boy. He'll let me know when he needs more than he's getting already. In fact, I think I have his hands full right now," Nina quipped.

Lamont just sat there with his head down. Nina guessed that he was probably just as embarrassed and hurt as she was at his mother's plain rudeness. Nina walked out of the house and waited outside. She wasn't going to subject herself to being talked down to. She wanted a fresh start to her life, but it seemed every time she took a step forward, something would make her take two steps back.

After twenty minutes, Lamont finally made it out. What followed was one of the longest, quietest drives Nina had in her life, as Mrs. Franklin somehow had both of them thinking. Saying absolutely nothing was far worse than saying something.

To make matters worse, when Nina checked her cell phone messages, her mother had called to say that she would be in town in the next few days.

twenty-six

Nina's job at the law firm was over by Friday afternoon. The woman she was filling in for had returned from her leave. Zohanna still had another week to go before her assignment ended. Nina was living with Lamont, had no bills of her own, and couldn't think of a better opportunity or time to invest her money in a business.

As they sat and watched a comedy show on television Friday evening, Nina told Lamont her plan. "I want to use the five thousand dollars and open up a spa."

Lamont looked at her sideways. "Are you sure you want to do that now?"

"What better time?" Nina said, sitting between his legs on the couch. "I can at least start looking at buildings or spaces."

Lamont gave her his undivided attention. "To save costs, you can travel to people's offices or homes."

"No, I want people to come to me. I want to see my name on the marquee," Nina said, sticking her chest out. "My name."

Lamont scratched his goatee as he thought. "Well, we can start looking. A small commercial space may cost about eighty thousand dollars in Brooklyn."

"That's not bad," Nina said excitedly as she turned around to face him.

"But there's decorating and design expenses. Contractor work."

Nina could tell he was running the numbers through his head. "You may need about two hundred grand."

Nina slowed down her roll. "Two hundred grand? Well, maybe it'll take a little longer or I can just buy a place that doesn't need that much."

"Okay, we can take it step by step. First off, we need to find a place. I'll give you the money."

"No, Lamont, I can't do that. I have to earn it on my own."

He looked frustrated and puzzled as he looked at her. "And how do you expect to raise that kind of money?"

"Aren't there bank loans? Maybe I can partner with someone."

"So I can't help out in any way?"

"Of course you can, baby," she said, kissing his warm lips that tasted like salt from the popcorn they'd finished. "But let me see what I can do."

"Cool," he said, running his hands through her freshly washed wavy tresses. "I want you to do what you love, however long it takes."

"It won't take long. I'll open this salon in a year or less."

Lamont kissed her nose. He loved her enthusiasm. "Or less. What if we did something else in a year or less?" he asked.

Nina just looked at him. She wasn't quite following.

"I want us to get married. Make you an honest woman," he smiled.

Nina wrapped her arms around him. "You want to marry me?"

"Stop acting like you didn't know." He laughed.

She played around like she was shocked, but she wasn't. She was just waiting for him to say the word. "Anytime, baby, anyplace."

"But my mother," he said, and both of them looked at the other for an answer.

"I need to have her blessings, Lamont. I can't marry you without that," Nina said, tracing the line of his thick lips.

He kissed her finger. "Why?"

"Because I am a woman with some dignity. I want to come into a family the right way. They say to know why something ends, look at how it starts. I want us to start right."

"Of course," he said, taking a deep breath. "What about your mom?"

"She'll be here on Friday. I don't know what for. The last time we saw each other I had a gun to my stepfather's face."

"I guess he had that comin', huh?" Lamont said with a pensive expression.

"Absolutely," Nina said. "I shot him in the shoulder, but if I didn't leave when I did, I might have ended up killing him."

Lamont's eyes withdrew when Nina said that. He'd never imagined that she even knew how to handle a gun.

"You think she's coming to make peace?"

"No, she's coming to get in my business. Maybe for money, who knows? Word gets around fast in that town."

"So why did you let her come?"

"Because she's my mama at the end of the day. And if there is a chance for us to make amends, I'm gonna listen," Nina said, massaging his shoulders. "But she probably won't."

"Do you think she'll like me?" He smiled.

Nina loved Lamont's vulnerability. With all his looks and charm, he still wasn't afraid to show his weak moments. "No, my mom likes everyone but me. And that's probably the only thing we agree on," Nina said as she cozied back into his arms.

At midnight, Nina and Lamont lay in bed as they ate gourmet caramel popcorn and watched a home improvement reality show. She had no idea until they moved in together that she'd find more things they had in common.

Lamont poured some deep red plum wine into her glass and his. Nina was always trying some new type of wine with him. Before Lamont, the only wine she knew about was the sweet wine her mother used to make Christmas cakes with.

"Lamont, I really wanna thank you for standing by me since I moved here. You've been with me 110 percent. You've given me a sense of stability and consistency in my life that I never experienced before," she said as she brought the glass to her lips.

He tucked a napkin under his shirt to catch the popcorn crumbs. "You're very welcome."

They kissed briefly, their lips tasting of the sweet caramel they'd eaten.

"I'm kind of worried about your mom," Nina said as the cheers from the television played in the background.

"Me, too," he admitted. "I had no idea any man hurt her like that."

"And that was so long ago."

"But after a while," he said, stretching out his legs before him, "much of that is self-inflicted pain. I think the pain makes her feel close to him. It's real sad."

"Was she with anyone else after my father?"

"Yeah, some men came and went. Mostly because she ran them off. She was never the same. The closest I saw her to being happy was when I first got married," he said, his voice trailing off.

"I see."

"And I think she'll be happy again when we get married. She wants grandkids. She needs to adjust, but I gotta live my life," he said, swirling the glass of wine in his hand.

"How many do you want?"

"How many can you handle?" he said as he cast his dreamy eyes on her.

"I can't wait to start a family with you," Nina said. "I think we would make great parents." Nina rubbed his thighs.

"Well, let's get started," he said, climbing on top of her. He sucked on her breasts, sore and sensitive to his touch. She loved her pleasure with a little pain. He licked and sucked every part of her like she was one of his delicious dishes. She slipped down to the middle of his thighs and held his cinnamon-colored length in her hands. She lapped it up like a lollipop, starting from the base all the way to the tip. He watched her tongue go in and out of her mouth. She sucked his dick, lick after lick.

Three days later, there was a message on her voice mail. She almost forgot her mother was coming today. Lamont had agreed that her mother could stay with them, and Nina made sure that the spare bedroom was prepared. She made sure she kept the hard, sharp objects out of sight.

"Nina, I'm at the airport. Waiting for you. Could you please hurry up? I'm at the baggage area. American Airlines." Nina's mother's voice was loud, clear, and frustrated.

Her plane had landed an hour ago, around 4 P.M. Nina rushed

into a cab to La Guardia during rush hour. Lamont offered to pick her up in his car, but he wasn't getting off for another hour. Most importantly, Nina wasn't quite ready yet to introduce them. She needed to feel her mother out, see what her visit was all about.

When Nina made it to the airport, Ms. Bettus was standing at the baggage claim area in a bright neon green jacket and skirt, one of her best church outfits. Nina was just so glad she hadn't brought Mr. Darrell, who hardly let her mother go anywhere without him.

"Hi, Mama," Nina said as she approached her with a hug. Ms. Bettus hugged her lightly and handed Nina a bag right away.

"Take this, will you?" she said, putting another bag on Nina's shoulder. "Do you have a car?"

"No, we have to catch a cab." Nina regretted passing on Lamont's offer to pick up her mom in the car. But her mom was too combustible to be trusted with new people, she thought.

Ms. Bettus huffed and cursed the entire way out of the airport until they finally got in the cab. She didn't stop complaining the whole hour trip back to Lamont's home about the flight, the food, the people, even the smell of New York.

When the cab rolled up on Lamont's tree-lined block across the street from Fort Greene Park, her attitude changed. "Is this where your new boyfriend lives?" Ms. Bettus said as she stood on the sidewalk while Nina paid the cab and got the luggage.

"It's where *we* live. Follow me." Nina opened the downstairs door, and brought her mother's bag into the parlor room.

"This is grand," her mother said, running her hand down the wood panels on the wall and admiring the open beams on the ceiling. "These ceilings are tall."

"Not exactly what you're used to. Huh, Mama?" Nina said,

waiting for a complaint. She counted down the minutes and one was about due.

"Why are the houses so stuck together like this?" Ms. Bettus said, peeking out the window. "I couldn't live on top of other people like that."

Nina ignored her as she brought her bags to the guest room down the hall. It was a charming, French country–styled room that Lamont had had designed by an interior decorator years ago. He rarely used it except for special guests. Ms. Bettus walked in and sat her big behind right on the edge of the bed. "Now this feels nice," she said, bouncing up and down.

"I'll take you on a grand tour in a couple of minutes," Nina said as she double-checked that her mother had a fresh roll of toilet paper in the bathroom. It wasn't so much that she wanted to play the good daughter, but she wanted to represent for herself and Lamont. When her mother got back home, she could tell everyone how much better she was doing.

"So how are you doing? Shot anyone lately?"

"I was fine up until now. I don't exactly go around shooting people. If I shoot, they deserve to be shot," Nina said firmly. "Now do you want to see the rest of the house?"

"No, I'll see it on my own time. I will be here for a few days. Where's that boyfriend?"

"He's at a client's meeting."

"What is he again? An accountant?"

"I'm sure Dee told you he is an attorney, Mommy." Nina wasn't going to let her mother push her buttons too early. She had to be stronger. "Thirsty?"

"I can drink something. I'll take a glass of Southern Comfort on the rocks," Ms. Bettus said, wetting her lips.

"I mean tea, juice," Nina said, her hands out in front of her. "You can come with me to the kitchen and see for yourself."

They walked down the hall to Lamont's gourmet kitchen. Nina's mother took a seat at the island where she couldn't stop her head from turning from left to right and back again. Nina smiled to herself, thinking her mama had already reached her compliment meter.

"No, no, no," Ms. Bettus said as she took a blue teacup that Nina had filled with water. "I do not want my water in the microwave. You do know how to boil water, don't you?" she asked, picking the teakettle off the stove.

"Yes, I do," Nina said, grabbing it from her. "And I'd appreciate it if you'd respect this house."

Ms. Bettus lashed a nasty look at Nina and took her seat back on the stool. The teakettle whistled when the water was ready and Nina poured them two cups. "We can sit over here," Nina said, walking to the large wood table on the other side of the room.

"You are gaining weight by the day. Are you pregnant?" she asked, blowing down on her tea.

"Excuse me?" Nina knew that was always a possibility, but she had been putting on weight consistently since she landed in New York.

"Your bones are built for a slim girl. You don't carry extra weight well," Ms. Bettus said as she sipped her hot tea.

"I am happy with how I look. My looks never seemed to please you anyway, whether I was big or small," Nina said, never remembering a time her mother even called her "pretty."

"Nina, I am not in a mood for your baggage. I need me some sleep," Ms. Bettus said, getting up.

"Be my guest," Nina said, happy to have a break.

"Good. If you don't mind, I wanna take a quick nap and help myself to some dinner when I wake up. You *are* cooking?"

"Mama, why did you come here?" Nina blurted out as they stood face-to-face in the kitchen.

"I came here because I wanted to see who this man was who Dee kept saying has changed you. But from what I can tell, you still pretty much the same ole Nina."

"And you're the same ole bitch," Nina hissed back at her.

"That's fine, I can take it, if I can dish it, baby. Takes one to know one," Ms. Bettus said as she rolled her big behind down the hall to the bedroom.

twenty-seven

It was Sunday. Nina and her mother had plans for church and brunch with Lamont. Ms. Bettus made Nina search all over Brooklyn for a church. Finding one wasn't so hard, but Ms. Bettus had all these requirements of the kind it had to be. Nina finally found a nondenominational church in Flatbush.

"I can't believe you just haven't been to church at all since you got here," Ms. Bettus said as they sat on the bus riding down Flatbush Avenue.

"Everybody doesn't go to church here. It's not like where you live," Nina tried to tell her.

"I really don't know what has gotten into you. It's like you can never be pleased. You left Trent, he died, and you still unhappy."

"I never wanted Trent to die."

Nina's mom didn't respond.

"Have you ever wondered why I'm so unhappy?" Nina asked her as the bus rumbled down the crowded streets.

"Nina, you are the only one responsible for your happiness." She looked out the window like Nina wasn't even sitting there. "Now, if you want to make me happy, there is something you can do."

Nina said, "What?"

"The house is going into foreclosure. I need about ten thousand dollars to pay three months' missed mortgage," Ms. Bettus said.

Nina finally figured out the motive behind her mother's visit. Her mother had mortgaged the house one too many times, and now the payments were too high. Nina would never turn her mama down, but she didn't have ten thousand dollars to hand over. "I don't have it."

"But I'm sure Lamont does. I'll let you work that out."

"Well, just like I'm responsible for my own happiness, you're responsible for your own bills. You got friends, family, and Mr. Darrell. You can't all put your heads together?"

"You just can't keep his name out of your mouth, can you?"

"No, not when I have to take the brunt of a problem that I shouldn't have to fix." Nina turned her face to her mother, who was still looking out the window. "Before I can even see how I can, we have to talk about Mr. Darrell."

Ms. Bettus's eyes grew small and narrow. "You are just hell-bent on seeing us break up. Well, if that's the condition you can forget it."

"To be such a lover of Jesus, don't you think you can at least try to treat me like I'm more than dirt? Like I mean something to you," Nina said.

Ms. Bettus rummaged through her purse and pulled out a mirror. "This just isn't the time and place. I understand that some things happened in that house that I dare not speak of on my way to the Lord's house. I just pray for you every night, Nina, I do."

Nina stared at the person's head in front of her.

"Well, if you're praying for me, please stop, because it seems like I've had nothing but pain," Nina said, hoping she'd take a hint that she needed her to talk to her, not pray. It wasn't about the money, but it was about a relationship she always wanted.

"Well, aren't you just the devil dressed in drag today," Ms. Bettus gasped. "I will never stop praying to the Lord." She made the sign of the cross over her. She used to do that a lot when Nina was younger. Nina just wanted a mother's guidance because from what she'd heard about her young life, it was three times the pace of her own when it came to men. Nina had to keep it all in, but like a dam, she was about to burst.

When they walked in to the Mount Bethlehem Church on the Rock, Ms. Bettus seemed pleased right away and fit right in with the white, wide-brimmed hats and big shoulder-padded jackets. Ms. Bettus walked in proudly holding her head up and her Bible to her chest. Nina did the same. She hadn't been to church in months, and this was one thing they could do without arguing.

Nina watched as her mother went into the aisles and did her hallelujah dance with some of the men and women of the church. They hopped, marched, and pranced up and down that aisle to the beat of loud, pounding organ music. It was amusing, and it was very much like home. Nina sat and fought to stay awake, while her mother praised the Lord on Sunday and talked about everybody on Monday.

After the service, it was like coming from the gym. Nina was tired, and so was Ms. Bettus, but the day was just starting. It was only 2 P.M., and they had a brunch appointment with Lamont at a soul food spot on Fulton. He wasn't exactly the church type. Lamont wanted to take them to a French restaurant on the Upper East Side in the city, but that would have given Ms. Bettus more things to complain about. She got along just right with sweet potatoes and fried chicken. Nina also thought it would be the right setting for meeting for the first time.

Lamont was waiting for them inside the restaurant when they arrived. Dark oak floors and wooden tables gave the place a comfortable, country feel. As soon as Ms. Bettus spotted Lamont, she had words.

"Is that your boyfriend? Jesus, he is about as black as you are," she said as she held a grin on her face and waved. "But handsome, very handsome."

"Lamont, this is my mama, Ms. Bettus. Mama, this is Lamont," Nina said as Lamont shook her mother's hand. Nina thought her mother had the nerve to act shy. Lamont looked a little smitten. Ms. Bettus looked good, as usual. She was a statuesque, beautiful, dark-skinned woman. The white dress with a lace inset made her look even prettier.

"Ms. Bettus, now I know where Nina gets it from. You look lovely today," Lamont said as he pulled out their chairs.

Ms. Bettus sat down first. "Honey, it's not just today, it's every day," she said, batting her eyelashes.

Lamont gave Nina a soft kiss on the lips as they both sat across from her mother.

"So, Lamont, you look like you could be a country boy. All strong and strappin'," Ms. Bettus said, slapping his hand playfully.

Nina smiled at her mother and Lamont. She was just glad she wasn't trying to start anything. But her mother was a sneaky one.

"Well, my mother spent some time in Houston," Lamont said.

"Where'bouts?" Ms. Bettus asked.

Nina threw a look at Lamont to change the subject immediately. She didn't want her mother to find out about how small of a world this really is.

"Oh, uhm," he said, looking back at Nina. "I mean, did I say Houston? I was thinking of Austin," he said, drinking his water slowly.

"Hmm," Ms. Bettus said, like she was lost for a moment. "Where?"

"Mama, you gotta taste the fried chicken and waffles here. They make 'em as good as they do back home," Nina said, pointing to them on her menu.

"Let me see," she said, slipping on her glasses. "Yeah, well, it ain't gonna be good as mine. I season my oil with slices of onion and fry my chicken in it after a sweet tea brine for twenty-four hours."

"You, too?" Lamont said. He waved to the waitress that they were ready to order. "I like putting a little bit of Old Bay seasoning in my brine. Cooking and food is my passion," he said, putting his arm around Nina.

Ms. Bettus's eyebrows rose slightly at that. Then she said, keeping an eye on them, "You know I used to use that, but I use just sweet tea, lemon, and salt. Come out just as good."

The waitress came just in time and scribbled down the orders. They all were having fried chicken and waffles. This wasn't Lamont's forte, but she respected him for going with the flow. If it was up to him, Nina thought, they'd be drinking mimosas and eating breakfast bruschettas.

After the waitress took their menus and left, Ms. Bettus asked, "So how did you and Nina meet?"

Nina jumped in to answer first. "Lamont and I met through my job. Right, Lamont?"

"Yeah, we did. It was a little tough because her job had all these rules."

"Rules?" Ms. Bettus asked.

Nina didn't want to get into the whole story about being fired. She was surprised that Lamont was just so quick with his tongue today. "It was nothing, you know how strange meeting people on the job is," Nina said to her.

Ms. Bettus frowned and looked around the restaurant. "New York ain't the kind of place where you just want to talk to strangers. That's why you meeting Lamont is quite lucky."

Something positive, wow, Nina thought to herself and decided to let Lamont take the floor. Lamont was the king of small talk and engaged her mother in some more conversation about food, recipes, and, of course, the church.

"I've always been a churchgoing woman. Everything I do, I do for Jesus. I don't need none of this world's praises," she said, reaching for her glass of freshly squeezed orange juice. "Did Nina tell you her husband was a pastor?"

Lamont scratched his bald head. "Yeah, she told me *all* about that."

"You did?" Ms. Bettus asked her.

"Yes, I did," Nina said, rolling her eyes, but she barely remembered if she mentioned it more than once.

"At first, I just thought he was jiving about being a pastor, but he did it. And he was real. God rest his soul."

"Excuse me, sorry," the young waitress said as she laid down their platters.

Nina's mother didn't respond as she stared at the waffles. "Are these waffles frozen?" she asked the waitress.

"No, ma'am. They're fresh. Straight off the waffle iron." The young lady gave them extra napkins and syrup and walked away.

Ms. Bettus cut into the waffle like it was oozing blood. "A fresh waffle is fluffy. This waffle tastes like a damn cake." But that didn't stop her from another bite, and another.

"They probably make 'em fresh, then freeze them," Lamont said. "You can never get anything fresh these days unless you make it yourself."

"Around my parts, everything is fresh. Even the women," she said, looking in Nina's direction.

"The chicken isn't bad. Not too salty." Nina sank her teeth into the juicy, flaky breasts. "This is good."

Lamont nodded.

"Well, for someone who don't even know how to boil water, you sure a food expert now," Ms. Bettus said. "The only thing you knew about cooking was to eat it." She laughed on her own.

Lamont winked at Nina as he poured more syrup on his chicken. He was telling her it was okay.

Ms. Bettus perched her elbows on the table and tore into that chicken like it was trying to fly away.

Lamont drove them back to his house and they sat in his backyard, a space he rarely used, but was handsomely decorated with ferns and an ample table that was the perfect setting for warm weather meals. They got back in time to see the beginning of a beautiful sunset as they sipped lemonade and Lamont and Ms. Bettus chatted. The comfortable August breeze left leaves flapping in the wind. Nina couldn't picture a better moment with her mother, mainly because she wasn't talking to her and Lamont was handling her just fine.

"This is just lovely," Ms. Bettus said, smacking her lips at Lamont's tasty homemade lemonade. "You live in a very nice place, a little smaller than I'd prefer, but it can work," she said, frowning.

"This is supposed to be a real popular neighborhood, Mama. All kinds of famous people used to live here." Nina tried to show off her New York knowledge.

Ms. Bettus cut her eyes at Nina like a backhanded slap. "Would you mind going to the kitchen and getting me some more lemonade?"

"Oh, I can do that, Ms. Bettus." Lamont stood up.

"No, honey, Nina can do it," she said, tugging gently on his arm so he would sit down.

Nina walked to the kitchen and refilled everyone's glass. She thought by the way her mother was acting with him that she may have been happy for her after all. She placed the glasses on the tray and brought the ice-filled lemonade back outside.

"Here you go." Nina handed one to her mother and Lamont.

Ms. Bettus took a sip. "This the *same* lemonade?"

"Yeah," Lamont said as he sipped, too.

"I'd like some more ice, please," Ms. Bettus told Nina. "It's *very* sweet."

"There's no more ice," Nina barked at her and sat down by Lamont, who knew he had plenty of ice stocked.

"Lamont, has anyone ever said how you look like one of those handsome movie star actors?" Ms. Bettus said, crossing and uncrossing her legs. Ms. Bettus had on a knee-length pastel-colored suit, but she hiked it up a few inches to show her thighs and knees. Her shiny, shapely, long legs were the color of Hershey chocolate. She looked like the model Beverly Johnson, but two shades darker. Nina knew her mother was a hot one, and she didn't mind. She just hoped to be that frisky at sixty years of age. *Hell,* she thought, *Lamont had said she had to get it from somewhere.*

"No, no one has compared me to any actors. But thank you. What do you think, Nina? You think I look like anyone famous?" he asked.

Nina just shook her head. "No." She wanted the evening to wrap up. She was on to her mother's game. She wanted to make Nina jealous to test out where her relationship with Lamont really stood. She'd done it before. "Actually, baby, shouldn't we all be getting ready for bed?" Nina said.

"So soon?" Ms. Bettus asked, seeming genuinely disappointed. "It's barely 9 P.M."

"But Lamont has work in the morning."

"He's a grown man. Right, Lamont?"

"Uhm—" Lamont didn't give a straight answer. He knew better than to answer that one.

"You and I can stay here and talk, Mama," Nina responded. "Because we need to."

Ms. Bettus said her "good night" to Lamont as she and Nina sat under the night light. No one wanted to start first. Nina's mother got up to get her knitting materials and sat back outside, on the other end of the table.

Nina knew not to disturb her mother while knitting and maybe that was why her mother chose to do it. But she was leaving in another day, and she needed to get a lot of things out in the open.

"Mama?" Nina began, not wanting to interrupt her concentration as she rocked back and forth in her knitting trance. "I can't ask Lamont for that money. It just wouldn't be right. We're planning on getting married and opening a business."

She stopped the rocking chair with her feet. "How in the world can you think about marriage when your husband hasn't been dead but for just a few months?"

"Trent and I were in a dead relationship for years. Haven't you heard about the problems we've had? How he was hiding all that money? How unhappy I was? On second thought, we hardly talked, so maybe you didn't," Nina said. "Lamont and I are starting a life here. And I really don't think it's right for you to ask me for money, especially because of how you treat me. I think you'll be fine, Mama."

"Honey, I've always been fine. I don't need your money or his money because you don't have any. Besides," she continued as she expressed some kind of amusement, "that Lamont is too good for you. He's too smart for you, too classy, and too good-looking."

"I'm going to ignore that because you want to turn this into a fight," Nina said in a composed manner, not wanting to be too loud outside with neighbors so close. "His mother didn't think that Daddy was too good for her." Nina wanted to hurt her mother as much as she hurt her.

"What's her name?"

"Her name is Grace Franklin, but they call her Lady Ann. She worked in the hospital and says she knows our family. So see, we aren't worlds apart like you think," Nina said as she folded her arms.

"Lady Ann? Why do I remember that name?"

Nina didn't care at this point. She figured they'd know about each other anyway, since they were all about to be family soon. "She said something about knowing Daddy."

"That is the same woman who killed your father! That old miserable leech, Lady Ann poisoned him," Ms. Bettus said with venom in her eyes. "How can you even think of marrying into a family like that!"

Nina didn't know that part. All the while, she was under the impression that Mrs. Franklin was just hurt by her father, but she had no clue that Mrs. Franklin really killed him. This was just an outright lie her mother mustered up, Nina reasoned. "You just don't wanna see me happy. You have to lie about Lamont's own mother. Don't you think she would have said something to him or to me if she had anything to do with his death!"

"No, because she is protecting herself. How can you be so naïve, Nina?" Ms. Bettus said in a pleading tone, reaching for Nina's hands. "You can't marry that man. I am telling the God's honest truth."

Nina believed her because her mother had never seemed more concerned for her than she did now. Just the touch of her mother's hand on hers was foreign. Her mother barely touched her at all. This was serious, and she knew it. "What am I supposed to do now?" Nina said, horrified. All she could think of was what to tell Lamont.

"What do you mean what you supposed to do? Get away from that Lamont and his wicked mother. I mean, despite all your daddy did to me, I never wanted to see him dead. When he died, our whole family suffered."

"Until you got with Mr. Darrell three months later," Nina snapped back.

"That ain't the point!" Ms. Bettus huffed, rocking the chair again.

Nina raised her eyes back to her mother's face. "What Mr. Darrell did to me has never gone away. So let's get to the real issue at hand, because Lamont's mother is another story. Did you ever believe what I said about what Mr. Darrell did to me?"

Ms. Bettus rocked the chair harder. "That is your side of the story."

"It's the only story!" Nina declared.

Ms. Bettus slipped off her glasses. "Darrell hasn't touched me in well over two years. Whatever he do outside our arrangement is what is keeping us together. You need to worry about your own."

Nina backed away slowly from her mother's coolness. She didn't understand how any of this was reaching her. "You're supposed to have my back, and not stab me in it with your coldness."

"I don't owe you anything, Nina," Ms. Bettus said. "Your father loved you more than he loved me. You took your father from me. I lost him years before he died. Then Darrell. You took him, too. You opened your legs for him like a street whore."

Nina felt a fire in her veins. She couldn't be strong anymore.

"Mr. Darrell raped me in your own house in your own bed," Nina cried. "Over and over. And I told you, but you didn't believe me. He made me do all kinds of things to him because he said you wouldn't. I hated him. I still hate him! He took every ounce of my hope, any love I had for myself. I would scrub my body so hard after he touched me that I'd be sore." Nina glanced at her mother sitting there wide-eyed. "I would've *killed* Mr. Darrell if I hadn't left that house. I dreamed of killing him. I still do."

The cold look on Ms. Bettus's face chipped away. She took Nina's hand again and put it on her lap. "I wanted to kill him, too. But," she said, breathing in deep, "he was all I had. I convinced myself that you made him do it. That was my way of—" she laughed awkwardly "—of making me feel better. I felt you had taken your daddy from me, and I wasn't gonna let you take Darrell. I knew what he was doing to you, and maybe that's why I need the Lord more than others. I couldn't stop it, Nina."

"Why didn't you at least believe me when I came to you?" Nina asked.

"I was hurt, Nina. I just couldn't up and leave Darrell. What happened to you was no different than what happened to me when I was your age."

"Then you should've wanted to help me. You were in my shoes before. I could never forgive you for that. Then telling our family how I was so dirty and evil for having sex with him, as if I was trying to steal him from you."

Ms. Bettus sat back on her chair, feeling defeated. Ms. Bettus's strong stance was gone. She looked older now than she ever had. Nina thought, *She's just as fucked up as I am, right now.* Neither of them had the answers.

twenty-eight

Nina's mother left the following evening. Nina had had her say. Ms. Bettus was who she was, and she had to accept that. Waiting for an apology from her mother wasn't even a question. She and Lamont happily saw her off at the airport.

Lamont was on Nina's agenda in the car ride back home. Immediately after they arrived at his house, she wanted to get into it.

Lamont quickly undressed as soon as he opened the door. It was 6 A.M., and he wanted to catch some more sleep before a late morning at the office. He donned only a fitted pair of white boxers that kissed his thighs in bed.

Instead of falling asleep, he first wanted to make love. It had been days because of her mother's stay, but she wanted to talk.

"Got your period?" He smiled. "You know that never stopped me. I just want a little bit so I can go back to sleep." His dark smooth lips planted kisses on her neck.

"No," Nina said, collecting the strength to tell him. She moved her neck away.

"Then what is it?" he said, sitting up. She had never refused him. "Is something wrong?" His handsome dark eyes consumed her long face.

"Lamont, I found out something awful. Something that I can't ignore."

Lamont flicked on the lamp on the nightstand.

"Your mother is the woman who killed my daddy. She poisoned him," Nina said, her shoulders shaking uncontrollably.

Lamont slid back down in the bed.

"Did you know that?" Nina asked.

"Nina, my mother may be a bitch, but she'd never murder anyone," he said, looking at Nina like she was being silly. "Who came out with something so ridiculous?"

"My mother."

Lamont didn't think it was so ridiculous anymore, but he wasn't about to let his mother be accused. "Maybe she lied?" he asked.

"Maybe she didn't! Didn't you see the hate your mother still has for my father ten years later? She had it in for him. She wanted to see him dead."

"I don't appreciate this, Nina," Lamont said, holding his bald head. "My mother isn't a murderer!"

"She killed my father." Nina trembled even though the house was room temperature.

"I think you better stop while you're ahead," Lamont said, jumping out of the bed.

"With pleasure," Nina said, getting out of the bed, too.

He seemed to feel the weight of the moment. "Nina, I can tell you don't want to do this. Listen, we can find out the truth together. Why flip like this?"

"I know the truth. The main truth is I wouldn't be able to

live with myself if I married you having to see your mother and thinking of my father's awful death. I couldn't deal with that," she said.

"So, you're just gonna walk out on everything we have?" he asked.

Nina sat on a chair, bringing her knees to her chin. "I think we moved into this too fast. I need time to think. I have to see if I can stay with Ms. Bauer and work this out alone."

"Well, don't let me stop you," he said, hopping back in the bed. He had had it with Nina, and he just didn't have the energy to figure her out anymore.

A couple of nights later, Nina was in her old apartment. She gave Ms. Bauer five hundred dollars from her savings until she worked out her next move.

She nestled in for a long, lonely sleep again. She smelled Lamont. She even heard his voice. She revisited the last few days' events in her mind's eye. She didn't want to leave him, but she thought there was no way she could reconcile her father's death. *Should I ignore it? Demand an apology from his mother?* She was too confused to even share with anyone. Then her cell phone rang. The person hung up. It rang again, and the person hung up before she answered. When it rang the third time, she picked it up and heard nothing. The person hung up in her ear.

The phone rang once more.

"Hello!" Nina shouted at the unidentified caller.

"Hey, girl, it's Zohanna. You all right?"

"Oh, hey," Nina said, holding her heart. "Somebody been calling and hanging up."

"Where you been? I haven't heard from you in days."

"My mom was here, and Lamont and I, you know how that is. Just a lot of stuff going on."

"Well, you tell him I said, 'Heeey,' " Zohanna sang.

"I will." Nina shrugged. "But not now. We broke up again."

"Come on now. Why?"

"I found out some stuff about his mother and my father," Nina said, not sure where to start.

"And?"

"My mother said she poisoned him. His mother killed my father."

"Whoa," Zohanna said, shocked. "Poisoned?"

"Yes, I loved my daddy, and I saw him when he died right in front of me. He choked to death," Nina said, her eyes watery with memories.

"Ooh, Nina, I'm so sorry." Zohanna's voice was kind and caring, exactly what Nina needed.

"So what did Lamont say?"

"He got mad."

"I don't mean to start anything, but I'd be mad, too, if somebody accused my mother of killing someone. How did you bring the topic up?"

"I just asked him," Nina said, wiping her tears with her pajama top.

Zohanna laughed gently. "Maybe it was the way you brought it up that got him heated or whatever. But you two need to work this out. Don't break up; it's the past."

Nina had never really been good about forgetting her past.

"What would your daddy want you to do?"

Nina hadn't thought about it that way. After a few moments, she said, "Kick his mother's ass."

"I feel for you, Nina. But this is the man you love. Just give yourself a moment before you do something you can't undo," Zohanna said.

"Thank you, Zohanna, I'll sleep on that."

"Good night."

A half hour later she woke from her nightmare where Lamont's mother was trying to kill her. She wrapped her arms around herself in the bed because she had felt a cool draft throughout the apartment. She wondered if Ms. Bauer had a bad window down here since she left. Nina walked to the living room and realized the window was open from the bottom. She didn't recall opening it at all, and she shut it as it was cold.

Nina walked back to the bedroom exhausted. She was glad it was 3 A.M. She had several more hours of sleep to look forward to. Then she heard footsteps. When Nina spun around, Ahmasi grabbed her by her neck and covered her mouth.

"Shut the fuck up, shut the fuck up," he whispered into her face as he held the gun to her neck. "I've been waiting for your ass to come back here. Your dumb ass makes it too easy for me. How you like living with your new boyfriend?" He grinned, his dreads looking wild and unkempt. He dragged Nina to the rear of the apartment and backed her up in the tub.

He kicked the door and slammed it shut. "By the way, who is that nigga? I mean, no one falls in love overnight. You had to be seeing him when you was seeing me. Fucking him, too, huh?" He grabbed Nina by the neck and pushed her against the bathroom wall.

Nina tried to pull his hands off her, but they were too strong, too powerful.

Nina could barely shout, as it hurt to breathe. "Please don't kill me," she begged.

"I wasn't, until you fucked me up again," he said, bits of his spit flying into her face.

"I ain't lettin' you go, until you tell me you love me."

"I can't."

"Say it!"

It wasn't until her face turned red and she began to drool that he let her go. He shook her by the shoulders. She struggled with him to get free. He pushed her down to the tub bottom, where he climbed in with her and pressed his body on top of her.

"I love you, Nina. So much," he said as he kissed her all over her chest. He pushed his hand down her panties.

She bit into his ear until she drew blood. He didn't budge. She wondered where the gun was.

"Please, Ahmasi," she begged. "Please don't do this to me."

"I wanna make love." He pulled down his jeans and the hardness of his dick poked at her. She wanted to die. He sucked on her breasts as she pelted his back with punches. His tongue ravished her mouth so hard she nearly choked on it.

"Get off!" Nina pleaded with him. "Please, don't!"

He stuck his dick inside her and bludgeoned her insides till she bled. Her body shook in shock.

Ahmasi began to choke her as Nina scratched his eyes. He reached to cover them as she grabbed the toilet plunger and knocked him across his face with it to get away. She climbed out of the tub, but he pushed her to the floor, where she banged her head on the edge of the sink. She drifted into unconsciousness.

twenty-nine

Nina was in ICU at Brooklyn Hospital. She smelled iron, bleach, and blood. She'd been in a perpetual twilight zone for the last three days. But in her unconscious state, she had heard when Amy, the lady in the next bed, died. Her unconsciousness connected her in new ways. She didn't know how she'd gotten to the hospital, but she was feeling awful. She felt like she had been punched in the stomach several times. She remembered Ahmasi, and what he'd done. She needed answers.

She opened her eyes. A nurse put her hand over her forehead. She looked fuzzy.

"Ms. Bettus, can you hear me?"

Nina could.

"If you can, please raise your right hand."

Nina did.

She paged the doctor, and he came right in. Nina's vision was clearer. The doctor was a short, slender East Indian man.

"Ms. Bettus, I'm Dr. Felix. How do you feel?" he asked, jotting down some numbers on a machine that was attached to her arm.

"Like hell," Nina said. "What happened to me?"

The nurse and the doctor stared at each other. When the nurse left, Dr. Felix said, "You had a miscarriage."

Nina squeezed her stomach with both of her hands. She had no idea she was pregnant. She couldn't have been. "There must be some mistake."

"I am sorry to say this but you lost your fetus. We usually advise pregnant women that sex is okay until the last trimester. But by evidence we collected from a thorough exam, you had very rough sex. You were assaulted, too."

"I was raped," Nina mumbled.

"Ms. Bettus?"

She had been pregnant with Lamont's baby and didn't know it. Her period wasn't even late. "How did I get here?"

"An older woman named Ms. Lorna Bauer."

"Is she here?" Nina could barely raise her voice.

"She said she was returning, but you have a gentleman here for you," Dr. Felix said.

Nina closed her eyes.

"We're just going to run a few tests on you to make sure you are as good as you look. You've recovered wonderfully from the minor surgery we did to remove the fetus, and there don't appear to be any complications, but we just want to be sure." He checked her vitals.

"Who is here again?" She could only think of one man.

"Don't worry, I will send him in," Dr. Felix said with excited eyes and walked out the door.

It was clear to her that she had made some bad decisions. She knew who she belonged with no matter what stood in between. Fate wouldn't have it any other way.

Lamont walked in. He looked withdrawn, but his clothes were creased and ironed as usual. He had a shadow of a beard, though he was usually clean-shaven.

"Hi," Nina said as he sat in a chair across from her. He didn't kiss her. He didn't say "hi" back. He just sat.

Nina waited for him.

"It's good to see that smile on your face," he said as he crossed his legs. "I was really worried that you'd be seriously ill."

Nina folded her hands and looked at the IV from her arm to the machine. "I don't look too good, do I?"

Lamont's eyes bored into hers. He walked to her bed and a tear cascaded down his cheek. He kissed her cracked, dried lips. That was love to Nina.

"The doctor told me I was pregnant with our baby," Nina said.

"Pregnant?" he asked in disbelief.

"I had no idea. I felt normal," Nina said.

"We were almost parents," Lamont said, stroking her dry, matted hair.

"Sorry," she said.

"Don't be sorry. It just wasn't meant to be to have a baby now," he reasoned.

"Lamont, tell me everything you know. How did you find out?" Nina asked Lamont, who sat on a small empty space of the bed.

"My mother is just a few rooms down. I passed by, and here you were."

"Your mother?"

"She had a heart attack when I asked her if she killed your father. She stopped by and I asked her. Still hasn't given me an answer."

"How is she?" Nina asked.

"She's in another room on the tenth floor. She's better."

"Oh, my God," Nina said, shaking her head. "This is insane. I'm sorry that happened, Lamont."

"Look, they're letting me take her home today. Now I just need to take you home."

Nina rubbed her parched throat. Lamont quickly poured some water from the dispenser by the bed and gave her a cup. "Thank you," Nina said, feeling frail. "Did they arrest Ahmasi?"

"They did," Lamont said, his face tightened with anger. "Ms. Bauer called the cops as soon as she heard the scuffling. He has no idea what he's in for."

Nina could tell that he was trying to be strong for her. "The next thing I knew I was being choked. He climbed through a window."

"I know, Nina, I know—" Lamont said, stroking her messy hair.

"He raped me," Nina finally said, her chest caving inside her. "Lamont, I can't take anyone else hurting me. I swear I will kill a motherfucker if anyone so much as touches me again," she cried, breathing hard and fast.

"Calm down, Nina, calm down." He rubbed her sock-covered feet. "You have nothing to worry about. I got everything you need to get better. We can start talking about setting up the spa. We can put all of this behind us like it—"

"What, like it never happened?" Nina said, taking a tissue from him.

"No, but maybe this is what happened to bring us back together. To make us see what matters. I don't know."

Nina breathed more slowly.

"I just know I don't ever want you to leave me again."

"And I never wanna leave. Never," Nina said as she kissed his wet face.

Moments later, the doctor returned and ran more tests. Lamont was by her side the entire time.

thirty

Nina had been out of the hospital for a month. She felt clear, clean, refreshed. She decided that in order to have a future, she had to let go of her past. Lamont had had no idea about his mother, and there wasn't any substantial proof that Mrs. Franklin murdered her father. Ms. Bettus had been known to make up a lie or two to suit her interests. It was no surprise to Nina that her mother had completely disowned her since she and Lamont started talking about marriage again.

But this week was Nina's birthday. She was going to be twenty-six, and she couldn't wait to put the last year behind her. On her birthday, Lamont prepared a small cookout for himself and Nina in the backyard. She had wanted to keep it low-key, and just have a calm, relaxing day with her man, Dee, and Zohanna. Lamont was all too happy about showing off his fancy grilling skills. Nina didn't care much about that. She was eager to finally show off her new man to Dee.

Lamont had fired up his grill with shrimp shish kabobs, steak, and juicy chicken pieces. They sat around his table where he had already laid out barbecue beef ribs, shrimp, steak, and chicken. On the side, he had seasoned French fries, arugula salad, and hand-rolled biscuits. For dessert, there was grilled sliced pineapple on top of French vanilla ice cream with rum syrup. He put his best foot forward as he wanted to impress her friends. What's more, it was her birthday and it showed he cared.

"Too bad you can't stay in New York any longer than a few days. I'd love to take you down to the Seaport. It's really nice this time of year," Lamont said to Dee as he filled up Dee's second bowl of grilled pineapple with ice cream.

"That cake looks gorgeous," Zohanna said, returning from the bathroom, her high heels clicking and clacking all about. "I'm not having another piece of chicken until I have some cake," she said, taking another piece of chicken.

"We'll be going inside in just a minute," Lamont said as Nina fed him a chicken thigh.

"I'm just glad I came to see Nina and that she is safe and happy. I hardly have time to travel, since I'm tied down to my husband and all his kids," Dee said, devouring the last piece of pineapple.

"They're not yours?" Lamont asked.

"I would never raise kids that bad," Dee said, laughing and smiling at Nina, who knew those kids were her blood.

"Tell me how Nina was growing up?" Lamont asked, giving Nina a sly look.

"This I have to hear," Zohanna said as she sat closer to Dee. "Was she ever a child?"

Dee laughed, then cleared her throat. Nina hoped she would keep her sarcasm and jokes at bay.

"Dee and I weren't that tight growing up. It wasn't until we got older, right, Dee?" Nina said.

"Please, girl. Don't tell me you gonna act all shy with that ole boy sitting here?" Dee said.

Nina took a few sips of red wine. She thought she was going to need it.

"Well, Nina was always to herself. Never talked to nobody, never had any friends but me and another girl. She got along with the boys good. Maybe because until about age eleven, she looked like one," Dee laughed.

Lamont flashed a quick smile for politeness' sake, but Nina wasn't smiling.

"I was real self-conscious about my looks, Lamont," Nina said, trying to clean up the awful picture that Dee painted. "I was a late bloomer."

"You got that right!" Dee said. "None of us thought Nina would have the guts to move out to a strange place, where she don't know a soul. But she surprised us all by following her dream. I mean, this don't happen every day where you land a man like Lamont and a good, solid relationship on your first run out the gate."

"Thanks, Dee," Nina said as Dee hugged her and kissed her on the cheek. Zohanna joined in, too. "I'm sorry you went through hell in between."

"All right, y'all. I'm not dead yet," Nina said, wanting to keep the mood festive. "I don't know about y'all but I'm ready for the next course."

"Again, Lamont, the food is fabulous," Dee said as she handed him her empty plate. Zohanna's and Dee's eyes followed his muscular arms picking up the dishes. He wore a short-sleeved, white cotton polo shirt and wide-legged, African-style khakis and moccasins. He always dressed well, and Nina knew Dee wasn't used to that. Men in their part of town wore their jeans like ankle bracelets and their T-shirts as long as dresses.

After dinner, they walked to the living room to blow out the candles on Nina's cake. It was a triple-layer red velvet cake with white, creamy frosting and chocolate letters. Nina, Dee, and Zohanna couldn't wait to sink their teeth in.

"The last time I had red velvet was when I was nine," Nina said, stealing some of the frosting with her finger.

"Let me get my plate ready," Dee said, laughing. Red velvet was one of her favorites, too.

"So, ladies, you think I can convince Nina to be my wife?" he asked as they gathered around the table.

"Lamont!" Nina said, pulling up her gold tube top. Something else had happened in the hospital. She lost at least fifteen pounds. She didn't know how he snuck that in there. She felt put on the spot.

"Girl, be his wife. If he can cook like this," Dee said with a laugh.

"Yes, we need a place to grub, for real," Zohanna said.

"None of you heffas will be up in here eating for free. I'm just being nice right now," Nina joked.

Lamont dimmed the lights and passed out three glasses of champagne. "Well, I have another question before we cut the cake and all," he said, walking over to Nina's side. When he passed by her, Nina inhaled his sandalwood cologne scent. He smelled as good as he looked tonight, Nina thought.

Then he whipped something out of his pocket. A sparkling ring. "Nina, will you be my wife?" he said, taking her hand.

Nina looked down on the fat diamond rock, and the light that shined on it nearly blinded her. It was an exquisite, round, solitaire diamond large enough that it'd be hard to hide. It was a jaw-dropper. Lamont had asked her to marry him. She hadn't expected the day to come so soon, but it was right on time.

Nina turned around to look at Dee and Zohanna, who had their frosting-coated fingers in their mouths, mesmerized. Nina looked into Lamont's warm brown eyes that were reaching deep into her soul. "Yes, yes, yes—"

Then he slipped the ring over her finger.

Nina inhaled a deep, full breath and scoped out her shiny rock.

Lamont kissed her lips lightly.

Dee got in between them and did a huge bear hug. Zohanna turned to Nina and gave her a bigger hug. "Girl, I love you. I'm so happy for you right now. But can we cut the cake?"

Nina and Lamont burst out laughing as Nina's eyes dazzled over the bright candles. They sang the "Happy Birthday" song, Stevie Wonder version, as Nina tried to keep her eyes dry.

"Make a wish," Lamont said, holding her from behind.

She closed her eyes and blew out the candles.

"Girl, I can set a small plate on that ring," Dee said. "What you wish for?"

"I'll never tell," Nina said, grinning.

Nina and Dee stayed downstairs in Lamont's place chatting the night away until 2 A.M. Zohanna had left a few hours ago. Dee had a 7 A.M. flight and it seemed like there wasn't enough time to catch up on everything.

"Lamont is so in love with you. If you snapped your fingers, you could get that man to do anything."

"I was pregnant, Dee, and I didn't even know," Nina decided to reveal. "I lost the baby when Ahmasi raped me."

"Oh, my God, Nina. I didn't know. I'm sorry."

"But how didn't I know?"

"Shit, I didn't know I was pregnant with Michael till I was in my third month."

"It's just so strange. Now I can't wait to start a family with him. That's the secret wish I made."

"Girl, he got some good genes," Dee said. "I told you once you find a good man, you just wanna give him some babies."

Nina sat there gloating in her joy.

"Nina, you are so fucking lucky," Dee said, moving her head up and down. "Have you talked about it?"

"Here and there, nothing deep. I think he will make such a good father. He's so smart, useful in the kitchen, and he loves me through thick and thin."

Nina stared into the diamond, and her future never looked brighter.

epilogue

one year later

Lamont and Nina moved to Long Island after they married. Nina thought that a more country environment was what suited her after all. Lamont was now a partner at Cromwell, Sutton & Franklin. Their lifestyle completely changed with his appointment. He worked from home all day and they were able to buy a multimillion-dollar home. They were also putting the finishing touches on a spa in Huntington that was set to open in three months. She planned to offer Asian therapeutic services, a skill that she had studied for several months. Lamont and Nina enjoyed cooking so much they even catered for Lamont's clients, mostly part-time or on holidays. They were still discovering each other and that was exactly what kept their bond as tight as it was. Also, three months ago, a lawyer had contacted her and told her she had money to receive as Trent's wife, based on his death. She got over three hundred thousand dollars in assets, which she chipped in with for the five-bedroom home. It made her feel good that she came into the marriage with something on the table. She was never comfortable being anyone's charity case.

Dee told her that Mr. Darrell got a local high-school girl pregnant. Ms. Bettus had given the girl a part-time job in the small jewelry shop she opened, and Mr. Darrell called himself "training on the inventory." Except the only inventory he used was on his body. Dee was practically her only connection back home.

Lamont's mother did not attend their wedding and she refused to speak to either of them. Her heart attack hardened her even more. This wore on Lamont, but every day he seemed to be taking it a little better.

Lamont wasn't perfect, but one thing Nina missed about him was his neat ways. Gone were those days. Nina did most of the folding, which wasn't so bad since he did all of the cooking. One thing she could do was trust him to stand by her. He had her back even when she was wrong sometimes. Whether it was standing up to his mama, the mailman, or the rude bus driver, Lamont always made sure she was okay. Last night he fixed her a fancy dessert of French vanilla, her new favorite ice cream, with fig sauce. Until then, she thought figs were just cookies. He rarely brought up the past and she thanked him for that. Even when they argued, he didn't throw her past in her face and she didn't his. If anyone were to ask him about it, that situation was written off a while ago in his book. But not to Nina. Sometimes she thought about Ahmasi and what happened on that awful night, and how he took the life of her baby that never had a chance. Ahmasi was serving fifteen years to life.

Yesterday, she found out she was pregnant. Lamont thought it was too soon to be called "Daddy." But something told her that this baby was here to stay.